enamoring her amnesic ex

a sweet romantic comedy

kristin canary

one

· · ·

OF ALL THE hospitals in San Diego, my sister had to pick the one where *he* works.

Fine—if we're being technical, she didn't really have a choice. Her water breaking in the frozen foods aisle of her grocery store wasn't exactly Theresa's plan.

But come on, universe. Did the closest hospital have to be *his*? I feel I have a right to be upset by this, but since I can't be mad at Theresa, here I am with the biggest bouquet of flowers I can afford (hint: it's not THAT big) obscuring my face as I slink down the brightly lit hallways. And you'd better believe that anytime I see a tall doctor with brown hair, I hug the wall like it's wool and I'm static, baby.

But I'm not letting a potential encounter with my ex stop me from meeting my newest niece. Because family trumps everything—even if being in the place where Dr. Kevin Bryant is a surgical resident is giving me sweaty pits and an itchy nose. Or hey, maybe that's the flowers shoved in my face.

Wiggling my nose like that girl from *Bewitched*, I book it in my jeweled wedges down the hall, almost to the magical door where Theresa and Jake await with their new bundle of joy.

And then, I hear it—that voice I'd know anywhere, even though it was only part of my life for five months.

And yeah, they might have been the most intense and wonderful five months of my life, but phantom whiplash still hits me when I think about them. Because all the intensity, all the wonder, came to an abrupt halt when Kevin figured out I didn't fit into the picture he had for his life.

Now, I can't help the yelp that comes from my mouth as I stop and peek through the flowers. My traitorous heart—which shouldn't care one fig about the man standing at the nurses' station after he broke my heart into a million pieces nearly two years ago—thumps a happy jig against my chest.

Down, girl.

Because he may have the same high brow, the same tousled dark hair, the same strong arms and lean body that suggest he still runs and lifts weights every morning like clockwork, but the harshness in his tone, the rigidness of his stance as he yells directives at the nurses and disappears behind a set of doors are proof that he's not the man I thought I knew.

My Kevin was sweet. A little uptight, yes, but considerate and generous. My Kevin would never treat people like that.

But maybe I just saw what I wanted to see back then. "Lola?"

I turn to find my brother-in-law standing in the hall outside my destination door, his brown-gray eyebrows raised. Jake's eyes are a bit red, probably from crying—he's a freaking waterspout, I tell ya—and his clothing is rumpled, I assume from the long night at the hospital.

Striding forward, I raise on my tiptoes and brush a kiss against his cheek. "Congrats, Daddy."

"Thanks. How's Sami?"

After Theresa went into labor and Jake joined her at the hospital yesterday, they asked me to pick up my five-year-old niece Sami from kindergarten and keep her at my apartment overnight.

"Wonderful and precocious as always." In fact, the girl asked me a million questions about birth and babies that started making me sweat. Thankfully, I was able to distract her with a Disney movie and pizza night. This morning before grabbing the flower bouquet I'm now holding, I dropped Sami back at school, where Jake will pick her up this afternoon so she can officially meet her baby sister.

"That's my girl." A grin sweeps his face and he pushes glasses up the bridge of his nose. Then he scans the hallway. "By the way, why were you standing there like Harriet the Spy just a minute ago?"

Note: Sami is obsessed with Harriet the Spy, so it's completely adorable that Jake uses it as a reference point in conversation. Not so adorable is the fact he caught my strange behavior upon seeing Kevin.

"No reason." I straighten and tug at the hem of my

aqua-colored blouse. "How are Theresa and Baby Girl? Did you guys come up with a name?"

"Not yet."

"All right, all right. You twisted my arm. I guess I don't mind."

"Mind what?"

"Sharing my name with her. Lola Warren's got a great ring to it, don't you think?" I wink and breeze past him. As I step inside the room, my sister's tired voice wades out from the other side of the privacy curtain—and an older voice responds.

Mom.

Ugh. Is it too late to escape? I turn on my heel, but Jake shakes his head. He juts his chin toward my sister's bed. "I need you to stay with her. Theresa's craving a breakfast burrito from Dos Brasas."

"Fine," I hiss out. "But I expect one too. As payment."

"Payment for spending time with your sister and adorable niece?"

I stick my tongue out—not so mature for a twenty-four-year-old, but when did I ever claim to be mature? "For forcing me to talk with my parents."

"She's already been on the phone for fifteen minutes." There's a bit of sympathy in Jake's voice now. He knows why this is hard for me. "I'm sure you won't have to talk long."

"Still, you'd better throw in a Diet Coke to revive my energy when you return."

He chuckles, pats my shoulder, and leaves.

Groaning inwardly, I brace myself for the inevitable.

Then I throw on a happy face and walk around the curtain, ginormous bouquet in tow.

Theresa's blonde hair is a bit grungy, tossed up in a messy bun on the top of her head—stay-at-home mom style, as she'd say—and her face is devoid of makeup like always, but the tiny smile lines around her lips are on full display as she snuggles her infant daughter against her chest with one arm and holds up her phone with the opposite hand.

When she sees me, Theresa turns the screen my way. "Look who's here."

I wave at the grainy image of my parents, who are squeezed in front of their computer in Zambia, where they teach English to underserved communities. Apparently they do a lot of good in the village where they've lived for more than a decade.

I hope so, considering what it's cost them—what it's cost all of us.

Stuffing down the bitterness, I set the flowers on the windowsill of the small room. "Hi, Mom. Hi, Dad."

"Lola! So good to see you." My mom looks older every time I see her on-screen—her hair a little grayer, the wrinkles around her eyes a little more prominent— but maybe it's just the terrible Internet connection. I wouldn't know, since they haven't been back to visit since Sami was about six months old and I've never been to Africa.

"You too, Mom." I move to the head of the bed, and Theresa flips the phone back around so it's fixed on her youngest daughter, who is sleeping and breathing in and out with an adorable little mew. At 8 pounds, 6 ounces, she's bigger than Sami was, though her legs are scrunched up like a little frog. Theresa has dressed her in pink footy pajamas that are just about the cutest thing I've ever seen.

Bending down, I kiss her sweet downy cheek, then the top of Theresa's head. "Good job, Sis."

"She's pretty great, isn't she?" My sister yawns and nearly drops the phone. "Sorry. Long night."

"We won't keep you, dear." Mom clicks her tongue. "Oh, I just wish I was there to hold my grandbaby."

"You could come home, you know." The words are out before I can call them back. I know better. Nothing is going to change. At this point, why would it?

"Lo …" Theresa warns.

Dad sighs deeply, taking his glasses off and rubbing his chin with a big meaty fist. "You know we would, Lola, but the people here need us."

We *need you*.

They're the words I've longed to say for eleven years since they left a thirteen-year-old me in the guardianship of my twenty-three-year-old barely married sister because their new life was "too unstable for children." But I don't say those words, because they're not true anymore. Nope. Theresa and I have learned to rely upon each other. We are all the family we need.

I force another smile. "I know."

After a few more pleasantries, my sister says goodbye and hangs up the phone. "That wasn't so bad, was it?"

"Torture." I tilt my head. "But worth it to meet this sweet girl."

Black-as-night curls stick out the bottom of Baby Girl's white cotton beanie with a pink satin bow. Apparently all Flanagan girls are born with dark hair that eventually falls out and comes back in nearly white blonde. At least, that's what happened with me, Theresa, and Sami. "Can I?"

"Of course."

My long hair falls forward over my shoulder as I gather the tiny bundle in my arms and get her situated. Her button nose and rosy lips remind me so much of her older sister, it's uncanny. "The Flanagan genes are strong with this one."

"Right?" Theresa pours a glass of water for herself from a pale pink jug. There's only enough to fill half her cup, and she downs it quickly. Then she relaxes against the bed. The room is small but thankfully private, and it smells like a mixture of baby formula and lemongrass. A large window lets in the morning light of another gorgeous mid-September day in San Diego.

As Baby Girl coos and inhales, I sigh in contentment. This is where I belong. With my family, who need me. I'll never regret choosing this life.

"So." Theresa studies me then tugs at the thin sheet covering her. "Did you see that job opportunity I sent you yesterday? You know, before I made a complete mess in Aisle 3." She hangs her head. "I'll never be able to show my face in my favorite grocery store again. Can you imagine the person who had to clean that up?"

"Oh, stop it. The staff will take one look at this sweetness and forget all about how she came hard and fast into the world." I run a fingertip along her forehead, tracing her cheeks, her nose. "Although maybe it wouldn't hurt to get them all gift cards as a thank-you. I'm definitely glad the manager acted quickly when she realized your contractions were coming so close together."

"Me too. And so grateful Jake made it just in time." Theresa, who is not the crier in the family, sniffles despite herself. "Find yourself a nice guy like him, Lo. It may have taken me a few years to see him as more than my nerdy lab partner, but now I find him the most handsome man alive. There's nothing sexier than watching him hold our daughters. Daughters. As in, more than one." Tears start streaming down her cheeks at an alarming rate. "Oh my gosh, I'm sorry. These postpartum hormones are something else."

I reach across to the counter and snag a few tissues, shoving them into her hand. "You definitely scored one of the good ones."

And once upon a time, I thought I'd done the same. From the moment I met Kevin at the diner where I still work—and accidentally served him a hamburger instead of his requested pastrami sandwich—things were like lightning between us. Hot and charged, yes, but deep too, leaving a lasting trench, a mark, on my heart.

Theresa blows her nose and then fixes her eyes on me again. "You didn't answer my question."

My nose scrunches. "What question?"

"The job opportunity. Did you look at it?"

"Oh." I kind of want to ask her which one she means, since she sends me several each week. But I'm not sure if she's in a teasing mood, given the sheen of tears still coating her eyeballs. "Um, no, haven't had a chance yet."

"Well, I think it's perfect for you. Assistant costume designer at a theater in Los Angeles." She straightens and I can tell she's about to go into teacher mode—I guess she can't help it after teaching science to middle schoolers for so many years. "Now, I know it doesn't pay all that well, so you might have to have a second job, but you're basically working two jobs now anyway. And this way, you'd get paid for the theater work. No more of this volunteer stuff. Which would be fine, but you have a bachelor's degree in costume design, for goodness' sake. You should be paid for your genius."

Baby Girl rustles and makes a sound like a grunt. *I agree, girl. I agree.* "It does sound like a great opportunity." I let my words trail off.

"But?"

"But you know how I feel about moving. I'm not going to be some distant aunt who never sees her nieces."

"Lo, Los Angeles is only a few hours away."

"I know, but—"

"And"—I hate how big-sister bossiness pervades her tone—"if you're ever going to go to New York and design on Broadway, then this might be a good step in the right direction."

"New York isn't happening, Reese." I try to infuse a lightness to my tone, as if my statement doesn't prick my insides.

"But it's your dream."

"Was my dream. In middle school. But now that I know what it would require … well, I'm just not willing to make that sacrifice."

I refuse to abandon the people I love like my parents did.

Like Kevin did.

Not for a million dollars—and not even for the chance to design costumes on the Great White Way.

As if I've somehow summoned her help, Baby Girl opens her big beautiful blue eyes—and starts to wail. It happens so suddenly that I jump, but Theresa just laughs and holds out her arms. "Saved by the cry of hunger."

Standing, I hand over the hangry monster who has replaced my sweet little niece. But as soon as Theresa has her suckling—like a freaking boss, I might add—she turns her pointed gaze to me again. "Now, where were we? Oh, yeah. About to dissect the trauma our parents unwittingly unleashed on you by sticking you with me as a pseudo mom. Is that about right?

"I mean, when you put it like that …" I tease.

Thankfully, I'm saved by yet another interruption when Jake waltzes through the door, a brown paper bag in hand and a soda. He wiggles them in the air and Theresa nearly leaps from the bed—but doesn't, of course, because I'm guessing Baby Girl would deafen us all if she unlatched. But when Jake places a foil-wrapped burrito the size of my forearm on the table in front of Theresa, she gives him the most solemn expression before saying, "I don't think I have ever loved you more than in this moment."

He turns amused eyes to me before handing me a burrito and the soda. "Do you feel the same?"

"Would it be weird if I said yes?" I grin. Living with him and Theresa for five years before living on campus at the University of San Diego for my undergrad gave Jake and me lots of time to perfect the brother-sister relationship. Even though I have my own apartment now, I still spend lots of my free time at their house, watching Sami and doing movie nights with my sis.

Theresa rips into her burrito, taking a bite and sighing with pleasure. The scent of sausage and cooked eggs makes my own stomach rumble, and I start to unwrap my burrito, which is warm in my hands.

"Do you have to work today?" Jake asks.

I freeze. Shoot, what time is it? My eyes land on the ancient clock above Theresa's head and the tension leaves my body. "Not for another hour." Which is good, because the lunch rush at Dom's waits for no one. Of course, I've told my boss that I might be switching shifts a lot in the next few weeks as Theresa might need me. And thankfully, the first costume fittings for *The Music Man* aren't until this weekend, so I don't have any set times I need to be at the theater until then.

Before I can even take a bite of my burrito, Theresa has inhaled hers, all while Baby Girl happily nurses. Jake is watching in awe of them both, and suddenly I feel like the thirdiest third wheel ever. I should be used to it by now—it's basically been happening since my parents foisted me on the newlyweds—but I still can't seem to escape the ick swirling in my stomach at the thought that I'm more an invasion than a help.

I stand, set the burrito on my chair, and grab the now-empty water jug from Theresa's side table. "I'll get you a refill."

"Oh, thank you. That would be great." My sister strokes Baby Girl's back. Both of them look like they're in a food coma.

Hustling from the room, I quickly find the kitchen area where the nurses stash little packets of crackers, containers of applesauce, and sandwiches for hungry mamas. There's an ice and water machine and I use both to refill the container to the brim. Once I set the lid on top, I take my time moseying back to the room. I stop to study a wall papered with children's artwork from the pediatric wing, smiling at the crooked lines and creative shapes.

"Lola?"

For the second time in an hour, someone is calling my name. But this time, it isn't my brother-in-law.

It's *him*.

And his voice in my ear is so unexpected that I shriek and jump, forgetting that there's a full container of water in my hands.

Liquid careens out of the top—guess I didn't secure that lid as well as I thought—and all over Kevin. As if that wasn't bad enough, I drop the jug, allowing what's left inside to spill out onto the floor beneath him.

Eyes wide, he's staring back at me with a look that likely mirrors my own. Along his strong jawline is a dusting of stubble, which is kind of a surprise given his propensity to shave every day. He always said doctors should present themselves as professionally as possible.

I lift a hand and give him the tiniest wave known to mankind. "Hi, Kevin."

"What …" He looks down at his green scrubs, which are drenched. Then his gaze moves back to me. "What are you doing here?"

The once-bustling hallway is now strangely devoid of people, as if the universe knows this moment is embarrassing enough. "I didn't come here to see you, that's for sure." I cross my arms over my chest.

"That's not what …" Kevin tugs at the badge on the pocket of his scrub pants. "Sorry. It's, um, good to see you."

"Sure it is."

Kevin shifts from one foot to the other. I'm shocked he's still standing here, to be honest. Maybe he's expecting me to go quietly like I did the last time we spoke. But I've got two years' worth of pent-up anger and hurt just begging to be unleashed on him. The only reason I'm keeping them in check? I don't want my sister's care to suffer. Not that a surgical resident would have anything to do with Theresa. But still.

Oh, yeah. And I guess I also maybe feel like he wouldn't care one way or the other. He was so clinical when he dumped me.

No feeling. No heartache.

It was so … *easy* … for him to let me go.

So sue me if I'm relishing his discomfort in this moment just a tad.

A pager on his belt goes off and visible relief finds the cracks in his face. "Well, I'd better go. I hope …" He swallows. "I hope everything is okay."

Dang it. There's a sliver of the Kevin I knew—the one who understands what it is to lose someone and works desperately hard so others don't have to. I can't leave him thinking that there's something wrong with my family. Or me. "Theresa had a baby."

"Right. Of course. That's why you're in this wing."

"Yep." My smile hitches one corner of my mouth at his logical brain at work. "Why are you here though? Doing a rotation in OB?" While dating him, I acquired quite the medical vocabulary.

"Just covering a shift for a colleague." He checks his watch. "Speaking of."

"Right." I bite the inside of my cheek, because the idea of saying goodbye … "Well."

"Well." His eyes connect with mine and spear me right there on site. I can't move, can't breathe. Their deep chocolate tones wash me in their sweetness, in the depths of what was. What could have been. If only …

Then the connection is severed when he pivots quickly.

But instead of moving away, he slips in the puddle of water that—until this moment—I'd forgotten completely about.

Apparently he did too.

His head bangs against a medical cart behind him. Before I know what's happening, his eyes loll back into his head and close.

"Kevin?" I drop to my knees, and my jeans are soaked in an instant—not that I care. He looks really pale, though I don't see any blood and his breathing seems okay. I pat his cheek but he doesn't wake up.

Turning my head toward the nurses' station down the hall, I cry out. "Help!"

A few people come running and they push me aside while I watch them take stock of the situation. They call for a bed and a woman in a white coat hurries over and examines him. It's all happening so quickly and my own breath is coming in short bursts. I clench my fists at my sides.

Finally, as they lift him onto a bed, his eyes flutter open.

"Thank you," I whisper as I step forward.

But the doctor gives me a side-eye. "Sorry, miss, you need to step back."

"Don't talk to my girlfriend like that," Kevin says before his eyes roll back into his head and he passes out again.

Did I miss the "ex" in ex-girlfriend? Maybe I'm the one who hit my head. And no, it's NOT wishful thinking, thank you very much.

The doctor and team start wheeling him away and I realize I'm biting my lip so hard that I taste blood. One of the nurses—a sweet older woman with a white poof of hair—puts her hand on my lower back. "We're taking him to the emergency department to get a full workup. Don't worry, we'll take good care of him."

And I do the only thing I can do. Because this is Kevin, and even though he is the absolute last person I wanted to see today, this is kind of all my fault and I owe it to him to make sure he's all right.

After shooting Jake a quick text, I follow the nurse down the hall.

two

· · ·

FORTY-FIVE MINUTES LATER, instead of heading to work, I'm sitting in the ER waiting room when Kevin's brother breezes through the door.

I met Connor when Kevin and I dated—he's a year older than me, and three years younger than Kev. And though he's a nice guy and they definitely look like brothers with their Greek noses and strong physiques, never were two siblings more different.

Where Kevin is fastidious and to the point, Connor is a lot more charismatic. A people person. And he's a commitment phobe—or was when I knew him, anyway. He dated a new woman every week, not wanting to be tied down. I think there's some hidden hurt in his past fueling that behavior.

And Kevin … well, he never dated. Not until he met me. And it wasn't because he isn't good looking or intelligent or generous or—

Stop it, Lola. You don't love the man anymore, all right?

You're over him. You're only here right now because you want to be sure he's okay. Now that Connor is here, you can leave.

At that moment, Connor locks eyes with me and his eyebrows lift. He must have come from his marketing job at a local publishing company, because he's dressed in nice slacks and a button-down purple shirt that makes his eyes pop.

As he weaves through the waiting room filled with people, I stand.

"Are you here for Kevin?" he asks.

"Yeah, I—"

"Wow. I didn't know you guys were back together." Connor leans in for a quick hug. All around us, there's a cacophony of noise. Babies cry, TVs shout the late morning news, kids play with the toys provided, intercoms blare.

"Oh, um." How do I explain the situation? "Well, I was actually here because Theresa just had a baby—"

"Wow, congrats, auntie." He flashes me a bright smile, and even though it does nothing for me personally, I can see why he's popular with the ladies.

I can't help but smile warmly back. "Thanks. Anyway, I was already here when the accident happened."

"Ah. I wondered how you got here so quickly. My job isn't too far away and I was in between meetings, so when Kev's co-worker called me, I was able to book it over pretty quick. Have they updated you yet?" His nose wrinkles. "Wait, won't they let you back there? Is that because you aren't family? That's a load of garbage. Come on."

Grabbing my hand, he drags me toward the ER reception desk before I can protest or tell him that no, Kevin and I are not in fact back together and that I haven't actually tried to get back there to see him.

The receptionist—a petite woman with platinum highlights and high cheekbones—glances up at us, then does a double take when she sees Connor. "Hi there," she purrs in a Southern accent. "How can I help you?" Her peppy timbre grates against my ears, but it seems par for the course when Connor's around.

I remember him flirting shamelessly any time the three of us went out to dinner. Even though Kevin and I only dated for five months, one of the reasons he chose to do his residency in San Diego—though he'd done med school in Texas—was to be near his brother, who had just graduated college and moved there from Los Angeles for his job after their mom died of breast cancer. So, we saw Connor several times and I got to know him quite well. When Kevin and I broke up, I unfortunately lost Connor's friendship in the process.

Connor leans against the desk and grins at the receptionist. "Well"—he glances at her name tag—"Michelle. My brother was taken back a little under an hour ago. He's a surgical resident here. Kevin Bryant?"

"Oh! I thought you looked familiar. Ya'll look so much alike." She giggled, then made a few clicks on her computer. "Why don't you sign in and then I'll take you back to see him."

With a flourish, Connor signs the clipboard she hands him. "Thanks so much, Shell. Can I call you Shell?"

"You can call me anything you want, sugar."

Oh, brother.

When Connor pushes the clipboard toward me and lifts the pen in my direction, Michelle's blue eyes flash at me, and I definitely wouldn't want to meet her in a dark alley. Sheesh.

"Oh. Sorry, I didn't see you there. Are you his girlfriend?"

I need to come clean on this once and for all. "No."

Connor laughs. "No, she's not *my* girlfriend, Shell. She's my brother's."

Ugh. "Actually—"

"Oh! That makes much more sense."

Wait, what does *that* mean? I'm not arrogant by any means, but it's not like I'm a complete ugly duckling who couldn't get a guy like Connor if I wanted to—and besides, Kevin is much more attractive. To me, anyway.

Why am I thinking about this? I'm not dating either one of the Bryant brothers, NOR DO I WANT TO! Never again.

Shell hands us two visitor passes and tells us where to go to find Kevin. For now, I give up trying to be clear about the state of my and Kevin's relationship—or lack thereof—and go through the double doors with Connor. We quickly locate the small curtained bay where Kevin is, but when we step through and find a doctor examining him, I stop.

What am I doing? I don't need to be here. This is a family matter. "Connor, I don't think I should be here."

His brow creases. "What are you talking about? He needs you right now. Look at him."

Kevin does still look kind of pale, and he's either asleep or unconscious. That can't be good, can it?

Still, I shake my head. "I just—"

"I need you too, all right?" Connor's voice is low and I have to lean in to hear it. And do I detect a bit of a tremble? He takes my hand and squeezes it in a friendly way. "Haven't been to a hospital since …"

He doesn't have to say anymore. I know how much his mom's death three years ago rocked his world. Kevin's too. I think it's why Kevin was so focused on becoming a doctor, to the detriment of all else in his life.

"Okay." I squeeze his hand back and his features relax.

Together, we step into the "room" and the doctor turns to us. "Ah, Kevin's family, I presume?" He's an older man with gray at the temples and tortoiseshell glasses. "I'm Dr. Shephard."

"I'm Kevin's brother, Connor, and this is his girl-friend, Lola."

At this point, I don't even bother to correct him. It'll all get cleared up soon enough. "Is he going to be okay?"

"So far all his vitals are completely normal and he cooperated with our diagnostic tests and passed with flying colors."

"Wait, so he's been awake?"

"Yes, he was only out for a few minutes after the initial incident. When he came to, he was naturally confused and complained of some dizziness and a headache. But that's nothing unusual with how hard he hit his head." The doctor pulls his chart from the foot of the bed and examines it. "All of that to say, we gave him some acetaminophen for the pain and he's resting now. We plan to keep him for observation for a few hours, but if all is well, he'll be discharged tonight."

"That's great news." Connor shakes the doctor's hand. "Thanks, Doc."

"Of course." Dr. Shephard pats the back of a chair next to the bed. "Why don't you sit and talk to him? I'm sure he'll be rousing soon and hearing your voice, feeling your presence, would be a comfort. I've got to look in on a few other patients, but I'll be back to check on him soon enough."

After he ducks out of the partition, I give Connor a little push toward the chair. "You heard the doctor. Sit."

Chuckling, he takes my hand again and tugs me around and into the chair. "I think he'd rather hear from you. Honestly, I hardly ever see the man. He's always working. I'm shocked you two find time to be together."

Okay, confession time. "We don't."

"Don't what?"

Someone's voice comes over the intercom, paging a doctor for a Code Blue. My fingers find the edge of Kevin's blanket and I glance Connor's way. "We don't find time to be together, because we're not together."

He crosses his arms over his chest. "I don't get it."

"Sorry. I've tried telling you multiple times, but we kept getting interrupted."

Blowing out a breath, he blinks. "So why are you here?"

"I told you. My sister had a baby. I ran into Kevin—quite literally almost." I cringe. "I'm the reason he's in this mess. I was shocked to see him and spilled water all over the floor and then he tripped and hit his head on a cart."

"Oh."

The air between us grows thick, and I start to rise. "I should go."

"No, no. Stay, please." He drops his arms and runs a hand through his hair. "Truth is, maybe this is fate bringing you and Kev back together again. He's been the biggest bear without you in his life."

My lips quirk. "I thought you said you never see him."

"I don't see him often, but trust me. When I do, he's not fun."

There's something just a little bit satisfying about thinking of Kevin being miserable without me. But then I remember that I never really knew him at all—not if he could throw me away so easily like he did.

I thought he might have actually loved me. I know I loved him, even though I never told him. Maybe that was the problem. Maybe we weren't real enough with each other.

Look what happened when I finally told him about my long-held dream.

My chest pinches and I sigh. "Whatever the case, I don't think Kevin will want me here when he wakes up. You should have seen how uncomfortable he was before he fell."

"What happened between the two of you, anyway?"

"You don't know?"

"Kevin just told me it didn't work out and to mind

his own business." Connor shrugs. "It shocked me because I'd never seen my brother like that before. I mean, how he was with you. Relaxed, carefree. Actually fun."

He *was* fun. *We* were fun, together. Memories pepper my mind like tiny grains falling on food, flavoring the past with spice and zest—hiking the Torrey Pines Beach Trail, snorkeling at La Jolla Cove, making out on the beach at dusk, when the sun was just kissing the sky goodbye …

My lips twist into a frown and I shake my head. "Fate didn't bring me here. Coincidence did. Nothing more."

Before Connor can say anything else, Kevin groans. His eyes flutter open and he squints at me. "Hi, Butter-cup," he creaks out.

The first time he saw me, he told me I looked like Buttercup from the movie *The Princess Bride*—his favorite. I die a little at the sound of his nickname for me on his lips. "H-hi."

And then he reaches over and snags my hand with his own.

Every nerve in my hand is singing, rejoicing at his touch. I hate every one of those traitors. But this moment isn't about me. It's about Kevin—about making sure he's well. "H-how are you?"

"Better now that you're here."

My stomach drops to my toes. "Oh. Um." I duck my head, then look at Connor, whose eyes are definitely bright with humor. "Connor came too."

"Hey, bro." But Kevin doesn't look away from me.

It's like he's drinking me in—the same way he used to. The way I never could get enough of. It's like his eyes know something I don't and it's their job to examine every inch of my soul, stripping me of every secret until I'm laid bare before them.

I used to love it.

Now, it's a bit unnerving—because Kevin doesn't love me anymore, if he ever really did. I can't trust him with my secrets. Not that I have any. But if I did, he's the last one I'd want handling them.

"Hey," Connor says. "I'm going to let the doctor know you're awake." Then he's gone in a flash, leaving me alone with my ex.

"Well." I stand, but because Kevin is still gripping my hand, I can't flee the room like I really want to. "You're going to be okay, so that's a relief."

Kevin struggles to sit up.

"Hey, hey, stay down."

"I want to sit." And he does, a triumphant gleam filling his eyes.

Something about the moment makes me laugh. "Why can't you ever just lie still for a moment?"

In one swift movement, he tugs my hand toward him, wrapping it around the back of his neck. Now I'm leaning over him, our faces only inches apart. The scent of his body wash—he never wears cologne at work— surrounds me and I've never found the combination of black pepper, basil, cinnamon, and amber so alluring.

"Because then I couldn't do this." Kevin takes advantage of my position and brushes his lips against mine—and I'm gone, transported to some moment far away. Time has rewound, and my mouth remembers what my mind and heart have refused to acknowledge.

Let's just say that chemistry was never mine and Kevin's problem.

Oh, sweet mother of pearl. What am I doing?

I yank away from him, expecting to see equal parts shock and awe in his face. But he just grins at me and tries pulling me back for more.

Thankfully, Connor and not one but two doctors come to the rescue. With the swiftness of a shopaholic at a Gucci sale, I scramble off Kevin's lap. Connor's look tells me he knows exactly what was happening in here when he walked in. I glare at him until he averts his eyes.

The new doctor, a redhead with a beard, claps Kevin on the shoulder. "Good to see you looking so well, my brother."

Kevin looks at him for a beat before responding. "Dickens, right?"

"What do you mean, right?" Dickens shakes his head. "How hard did you hit your head?"

"Pretty hard if the spinning lights are any indications." Kevin squints. "But when did you grow a beard?"

The man glances at Dr. Shephard, his eyebrows slanted, before looking at Kevin again. "I've had a beard for the last eighteen months. Where have you been?"

Kevin chuckles and there's something loose in it. He's not at all uptight like he was when I saw him earlier in the hallway. What's going on with him? "Come on, man. Quit fooling. I saw you just last week and there wasn't a single hair on your face. You keep it as clean as I do." He runs his hand down his own stubbled jaw, then frowns. "I know I shaved this morning. How weird."

He shifts to the edge of the bed and addresses Dr. Shephard. "I'm sorry for all the trouble. This is really embarrassing." Kev offers a wry grin. "I promise I'll spend the next six years proving to everyone at this hospital that I'm not really such a klutz."

Six years? I can't help but voice my confusion. "I thought your residency was only six years long." And he's already two years in.

He looks at me like *I'm* the one not making sense. "That's why I just said I'd spend the next six years proving my worth."

"Wait." Connor holds up a hand and glances between the doctors, me, and Kevin. "How far into your residency program are you?"

Kevin's eyes narrow. "What are you talking about? You know I just started a week ago."

My knees buckle and I lean against the chair for support as Connor and the doctors ask a few more questions: What year is it? Who is the President? What was the last thing Kevin remembers?

All of his answers—given so matter of factly, with not an ounce of wavering—point to one obvious conclusion.

Kevin thinks it's two years ago.

Two years ago, we had been dating for three months. We hadn't said I love you yet, but I already knew I wanted to spend the rest of my life with him.

And maybe that seems quick, but sometimes you just know.

At least, I thought I knew.

Two years ago, we were happy—and had no idea that heartbreak was only a few months away.

three

. . .

"AMNESIA?" My sister's shrill voice would wake the dead, but Zoe—Baby's Girl name as of last night—remains asleep in her bassinet next to Theresa and Jake's couch.

"Yes." I groan as I plop onto the couch beside her with a bowl of cereal. Sure, it's noon on a Thursday, but what can I say? I eat when I'm stressed. I really do go cuckoo for Cocoa Puffs. "Of all the cosmic jokes in the world, this one has to be the cruelest."

"I'm sorry, sis." Theresa yawns as she leans her head against the back of the couch. Poor woman. They weren't discharged until late last evening, so I picked up Sami from the hospital room yesterday afternoon—a welcome reprieve from the Kevin situation—then brought her back to her own bed.

Once Jake and Theresa arrived home from the hospital, I spent the night, having a midnight party with Zoe watching *Legally Blonde* so Theresa could rest. I may have had a little chat with my new niece about the importance of finding herself an Emmett, NOT a Warner.

Then I might have—maybe just a little—replayed that kiss from Kevin in my brain over and over again.

Along with the conversation that Connor and I had with the doctors afterward.

The one I'm finally talking with my sister about, now that we are both awake.

"What did Kevin say when you told him?"

Wincing, I crunch the cereal between my teeth. But not even the glorious taste of highly processed chocolate on my tongue can counter the bitterness of the situation in which I find myself.

My silence tells her everything.

"Lo." She leans toward me, like I imagine a mother duck watching her new duckling wade into the water—alert and ready to rescue him should he start to drown. "What did he say?"

"We didn't tell him." Quickly, I shove another bite of cereal into my mouth. Some milk dribbles down my chin and I swipe at it with the sleeve of my sweatshirt.

"And just why not?"

"The doctors said it would be good to ease him into the news. They wanted to spend the day running a few extra tests."

"As a doctor, didn't he find that suspicious?"

"He was pretty out of it all day with some pain and light sensitivity, and kind of confused too. Connor said he didn't ask many questions." Which totally wasn't like Kevin.

Theresa studies me while she absently fiddles with the strap of her cotton pink nursing shirt. "When are they going to tell him?"

"As Kevin's temporary health proxy, Connor decided to hold off on telling Kevin about his amnesia until he's had some time to physically recover. He promised to be in close touch with the doctors, and since Kevin is a resident there, they supported his decision. Connor is going to deliver the news in the comfort of Kevin's own home."

And he wants my help doing it—not that I'm telling Theresa that, though.

But like the mom and teacher she is, the woman has some sort of Spidey sense when I'm not telling her the complete truth. She always has, which made sneaking out in high school basically impossible. "So your part is done, right?"

"Well …" Another bite and my cereal is gone. All that's left is the chocolate milk in the bowl. Ignoring the probing look pointed my way, I slurp it down.

"Lola Flanagan, are you seriously considering getting involved with him again?"

I choke on the milk, which gets caught in my throat. "What? No!" Sighing, I place the bowl in my lap. "Connor wants me to come over today to help him tell Kevin the truth. He thought it would be better to do it at home than in the sterile hospital environment."

"And just why do *you* have to be there?"

Waving my spoon at her, I narrow my eyes in what I hope is an intimidating don't-mess-with-me look—but likely more resembles a petulant I-don't-want-talk-about-it. "You sound like Mom right now. You should really cut that out."

"Someone has to talk sense into you."

"Look, I'm basically responsible for his fall."

"It was an accident."

"Still." Standing, I move to the kitchen to place the bowl and spoon into the dishwasher—and breathe in some fresh air. But there's no escaping my sister, who follows me with the grunting patter of someone who just pushed a large baby out not even forty-eight hours ago. She really should be sitting or lying down.

But before I can suggest it, she continues the conversation I don't want to be having. "How long is this amnesia supposed to last?"

Flicking on the water, I fill the bowl. "The doctors couldn't say. According to Connor, the tests all came back fine, so it could be any time." Even though it's totally unnecessary, as there aren't any bits of food stuck to it (I made sure of that), I take a scrubber to the inside of the bowl. "There are therapies that could help him regain his memories, but for now they just want him to rest and see if the memories come back on their own."

And the sooner, the better, honestly. I'm not sure I can take a version of Kevin who looks at me the way he did yesterday—like I'm the sun to his moon, the chocolate to his peanut butter, the silk to his wool.

Theresa hovers to my right. "So you're just going to tell him today and then wash your hands of him, right?"

"That's the plan." Thanks to the violence of my scrubbing, water splashes up onto my sweatshirt. I stop and inhale. The kitchen smells of cinnamon, and I'm transported back to that hospital bay, back to Kevin's arms. And that's when I drop the scrubber and brace myself with both forearms against the counter. "It was like I had him back, Reese. For a brief few minutes, it was like nothing had changed between us at all. He wasn't pushing me away—he was holding me close. And …"

Ugh. My eyes burn.

"Shhh." She pulls me to her and I hang on tight, forcing the tears that want to fall to stay put. Because I will not cry over this man again. I won't. I've spent too many tears already.

Theresa pulls back and keeps one hand on my shoulder. The other she uses to play with the ends of my hair in that comforting way that mother figures do. "You can say no, you know. You don't have to go over there today. Why torture yourself?"

"I told you. It's my fault."

"There's more to it than that and you know it." She cocks her head. "Do you think maybe some part of you is hoping for a second chance?"

"No." That much is for sure. Because I know what will happen when Kevin regains his memories. He will remember how much better his life is without me—it has to be, right? Because for nearly two years, I haven't heard a word from him. "I think I just need to prove to myself that I'm over him."

"Are you sure that you are? Given this reaction—"

"It was just shock, that's all." I grip her hand and squeeze.

"He broke you, Lo. I don't want that to happen again."

"I'm not broken."

"That's not what I mean." She sighs. "But you stopped reaching for your dreams after that. You had these big plans to do grad school in New York and then you just … never applied."

She's not wrong, though that wasn't the only reason I stayed put. I can't tell her the other reason—her. I still remember her words one night a few months after Sami's birth: *"I couldn't have done this without you."* She'd been exhausted from late-night wakings and some postpartum anxiety that had taken hold. Then she said the same thing again a year and a half ago, after an unexpected miscarriage.

Knowing that, I'm determined that she won't have to do Zoe's early months alone either.

But if I tell her that, she'll think she's holding me back. In reality, I've just fully realized what's important. I've always known it, what with my parents' early exit from my life, but the last few years have really solidified that knowledge.

I'm needed here, and that means I can't go to New York. I've made peace with that. I'm even mostly happy about it. Really.

I clear my throat. "I'll be careful, okay? I promise."

From the other room, Zoe cries and Theresa's chest is wet in an instant. She glances down and groans. "Dang it. I forgot to put nursing pads in my bra. The joys of motherhood."

"You're a good mama." To Zoe, to Sami—and, in a way, to me.

"I love all my babies." She looks at me and I feel that love in every fiber of my being.

"I know."

I also know she just wants to protect me from getting hurt again. But I'm stronger now. Kevin doesn't have any hold over my heart.

Not anymore.

Just because Kevin doesn't own my heart anymore doesn't mean I'm not going to do my best to show him what he's missing.

Though I don't design my own clothes (I save all my creative energy for the stage), I still have a style I prefer: bright clothes, heels or wedges whenever possible, blouses with funky patterns, and chunky jewelry.

Today I'm sporting a skirt (Kevin maaaaay have once upon a time told me he was a sucker for a great pair of legs), a hot pink off-the-shoulder blouse, and canary-yellow hoop earrings, all finished off with natural-looking makeup and curled hair.

You know—the basic eat-your-heart-out-but-oh-wait-you-can't-because-you-dumped-me look.

I adjust my purse strap and knock on Kevin's apartment door. It's been six hours since my chat with Theresa and that's given my nerves plenty of time to settle. If only they would listen to my repetitive "this is the last time you ever have to see this man" speech. The plan is to get in, help Connor tell Kevin the truth, and get out—then head back to my house. I offered to be on Zoe duty tonight, but Jake's mom beat me to it, so I'll probably head to the theater for some costume work after this. Depending on how it goes here, I may stop at the store to grab my good friends Ben and Jerry and bring them along.

Connor opens the door. "Thanks for coming." He glances back and lowers his voice. "Kev is feeling better, but no return of memory yet that I can tell."

"All right." I shift my weight from one foot to the other. "How do you want to play this?"

"Maybe we ease into it? The doctor said to make sure he felt well enough physically. Kev hates to admit when he's in pain, so he's pulling the big brother tough act with me. But maybe he'll let down his defenses with you."

I frown. "I don't want to lie to him. Isn't it better to just rip off the Band-Aid?"

His fingers drum along the edge of the door. "We could, I guess. I was just going with what the doctor suggested."

"No, that makes sense." Inhaling a shaky breath, I gnaw at my lip. "I'm honestly surprised they don't need to be here for it."

"I kind of was too, but they said in their experience, news like this is best delivered by people the patient trusts." He looks at me.

Guess that's why I'm here.

Connor continues. "Besides, they know Kevin. The second he learns about this, he will be back at the hospital drilling them for answers."

"That's definitely true." And that will give them a chance to go over the pertinent information then. I square my shoulders. "All right. Let's just get this over with."

"Hey, I know this has to be awkward for you. I really appreciate it." He kicks at the worn hallway carpet. Kevin's actual apartment is nice inside, but everything in California is expensive and he's still living on a resident's salary and paying off loans. "The last sick person I was around was Mom. I'm not exactly the nurturing type. Sick people kind of freak me out."

"Is your dad coming down to help?"

"Nah, couldn't get away from work." Their father is a big-time surgeon in LA. "But that's probably better for all of us."

"No argument here." The one and only time I met Robert Bryant, he spent the entire dinner berating Connor for not going into medicine like his big brother and discussing all the reasons Kevin should have taken him up on his offer of a prestigious residency at *his* hospital.

"Is that Lola?" Kevin calls from inside the apartment.

Connor raises his eyebrows at me. "Showtime." He steps aside so I can enter.

Kevin's apartment is exactly as I remember it. Stark white walls except for one abstract picture I bought for him at a farmer's market that adds pops of color to the room. A big-screen TV mounted on the wall opposite the sturdy black couch where Kevin is currently lying. No dust anywhere. Nothing out of place.

The whole space smells like it was sprayed with Kevin's body wash. Not in a cloying way, like a teenage boy going on his first date, but in a way that settles in every nook and cranny.

My gut twists at the sight of this time capsule of an apartment, where so many memories were made. Nothing necessarily life altering or significant—just lots of little moments that amounted to something deep.

My whole body is humming with them.

Gah. This is not good. *Abort, abort!* Good Sense Lola is screaming at me to make up an excuse and get the heck outta here.

But does my heart listen to my good sense? No. No, it does not.

"Hey." My voice is breathy and catches in my throat.

Smiling, Kevin sits up and holds out his arms. "I've been looking forward to this all day."

With a nervous glance at Connor, who is staring at the ground, I move toward Kevin and sit beside him, allowing him to envelop me in his embrace. His strong arms come around my waist and squeeze the resistance out of me. Except, I can't let that happen, not again. I have to be stronger today than yesterday when he kissed me—a mantra for my life if I ever heard one.

Pulling away, I scooch back and tuck the edges of my skirt under my thighs. This seems to be a bad move, though, because it draws Kevin's attention downward. "I don't think I've seen this outfit. Is it new?" He thumbs the material, his fingers skating to my left knee —and staying there.

I shiver at the casual touch. "Um, no. Not new." I got it about a year ago from a thrift store that I drag Theresa to sometimes. "How are you feeling?"

Connor takes that opportunity to duck into the kitchen, probably so Kevin will answer honestly.

It seems to work, because Kevin—who is sitting sideways, facing me—places his free arm along the back of the couch and leans his head against it. "Been better." He starts fiddling with my earring in a gentle way, and I both want to lean into it and pull away. "My head is still hurting and I've had some bouts of nausea. All totally normal for a concussion. Don't worry."

My nose scrunches. "Why do you think I'm worried?" I'm not.

I'm NOT.

"Because you have your worried face on."

"I have a worried face?" He's never mentioned it before. But I kind of love that he knows this about me.

Kevin's hand lifts off my knee—thank goodness, as the burning heat was about to sear all the way through to the couch—and moves to the edge of my eye. "You have these two lines that appear here"—he strokes the groove just outside my eye—"and here." His thumb grazes a trail along my forehead.

I swallow against a dry throat. "Oh."

"But I can always tell because those beautiful lips of yours dip downward." He leans in closer, and I swear my rear is glued to this freaking couch. It ain't moving no matter how much I will it to. "And I'd do anything to turn them right side up."

He's a hair's breadth away from kissing me again and I just sit there, almost like my body wants what my heart does not—*bad Lola!*—when Connor re-enters the room and saves me. "Whoa, sorry there, lovebirds."

Kevin sighs and turns to glare at his brother. "Don't you have somewhere to be? Lola's here now, and she'll be the best nurse possible."

I turn wild eyes on Connor. He wouldn't leave me.

"I'm sure she would." Thankfully, Connor has heard my silent pleas—or threats—and rounds the couch to sit in Kevin's recliner near the window. The sun is almost completely retired for the day. Is it already so late? We need to get this show on the road. "But I'm here to make sure you actually rest and don't just make out all evening."

Darn Connor for putting such ideas into my brain— or Kevin's. But I jump at the chance to escape. "Connor's right." Standing, I race to the kitchen for an ice pack and a glass of water. When I return, I eye Kevin and point to the part of the couch where he was lying before. "Back down."

"Only if you join me." He winks, then grimaces, which I take to mean his head is still aching.

"No more sitting up, and I mean it."

"Anybody want a peanut?" Oh, boy. Now he's quoting *The Princess Bride*, a movie we must have seen together twenty times in the last few months that we dated. Kevin used to watch it with his mom as a kid, and it was his favorite way to wind down after a crazy day at work. After we shared takeout, I would lie with my head in his lap while we watched. He'd stroke my hair. And half the time, I'd fall asleep on him and wake up the next morning on the couch with a blanket over me and a note telling me the coffeepot was set—all I had to do was hit Brew.

I can't help the laugh that bubbles out of me as Kevin grins and complies with my request. Then I lower myself onto the edge of the couch beside him, set the water on the coffee table, and place the ice pack over Kevin's eyes.

And FINE. Maybe I allow my fingers to brush through his hair before I remove them. I cannot be blamed. It's just pure instinct.

He grabs my hand before I can move away completely. "That feels nice. Can you do it some more?"

He doesn't know what he's asking of me. If he did, it would be cruel.

Without replying, I do as he asks, and his whole body relaxes. Meanwhile, my own stiffens. The recliner squeaks a little as Connor rocks, and when I glance at him, he's staring at me intently. What must he think of me, of this situation? Does he know that it's killing me to be here, to have my Kevin back … but for how long?

I pull my hand away. "Maybe … maybe I should make us some dinner. How would that be?"

Kevin removes the ice pack to look at me. "*You* want to cook?" he says in a teasing tone.

"Hey." I smack his upper arm lightly. "I've gotten much better in recent years."

"I'd hate to have tasted *that,* considering you burned the lasagna just last week."

The reminder of our reality—that he's two years in the past—slams into me.

He must sense my discomfort because he reaches for my hand. "You know I'm just kidding. It's not like I can cook either." He glances at Connor and smiles. "Only one of us got the cooking gene from Mom, and it wasn't me."

"You got the Best Son gene, though." Connor chuckles, but there's something tense in it.

Kevin either doesn't notice or just ignores Connor's self-deprecating remark and turns his attention back to me. "Besides, you've got so many other talents that are way better than cooking." He waggles his eyebrows and lowers his gaze to my lips.

My cheeks heat, but I pretend to be affronted instead of embarrassed. "If you're not going to behave, I'm leaving." I start to stand and he snatches my wrist.

"I meant your design work. What did you think?" He grins. "How's the show going, by the way? You're not having to miss rehearsal because of me, are you?"

How does he know I'm doing a show? I plop back beside him. "No."

"That's a relief. I wouldn't want to bring Bob's wrath upon my head. From what you've told me, he doesn't sound like a good guy."

Bob? Oh yeah. Bob Scafferty, the director of *Beauty & the Beast,* the show I was working on in Kev's remembered timeline. Bob has since moved on to better pastures, and I like his replacement Debra much better. "You don't have to worry about him."

"Do you have pictures of the costumes yet?" The pride in his voice guts me. Was he always this supportive of my work?

"You want to see them?" I think I showed him a few idea sketches for the musical but he never saw the real thing.

Because he dumped me right before the show.

The thought tastes sour in my mouth. I really should be going. I have a feeling that Kevin isn't ready to hear the truth about his amnesia yet—he's yawning and it's clear he's in pain, despite his chattiness—so it's doing absolutely no good for me to be here.

Just as I'm about to announce my departure, Connor's phone rings. He fishes it out of his pocket. "Hello?" His relaxed face tightens and he groans. "Are you sure?" A pause. "I can't—" Another groan. "Hang on a sec."

Lowering the phone and covering the receiver, he looks at me. "I'm so sorry to do this, but there's a work emergency and I have to go in. Would you mind staying here tonight? There's no telling how long it will take and …" He looks at Kevin, who is already asleep.

"He can't be alone?"

"The doctor recommended we stay with him for the first several days while he rests up and … gets his bearings. We don't want his confusion to get out of control. If he tried leaving the apartment before he knows the truth, that wouldn't be good."

There goes my chance to make any progress on The

Music Man costumes. But after the last few days, maybe going to bed early and watching some TV wouldn't be a terrible thing.

Besides, Kevin seems like he's down for the count. I probably won't need to do more than leave him a note so he'll know I'm here if he wakes up in the middle of the night. "Fine."

"Thank you, Lola." Connor hops up and rushes toward the door. "You're the best."

"Wait. When will you be back?"

"I'll come by in the morning to make breakfast. Maybe we can tell him then. You just hold down the fort tonight. Hopefully he sleeps like a baby and you won't have to do anything. Just being here is enough."

"You know, babies don't actually—"

Before I can finish my thought, he's gone and I'm left alone once again with my ex. If I didn't know any better, I'd think Connor was doing this on purpose, but the panic in his eyes at that phone call was real.

Sighing, I replace the ice pack on Kevin's head and pull a blanket over him. He's definitely out, so I take the opportunity to walk to his kitchen and grab something to eat. When I glance inside, I see a tub of spring mix that looks slightly wilted, a wrinkly apple, a carton of expired milk—though only by a few days—and several takeout containers.

Wow. Kevin's eating habits have definitely gone downhill. Even if he wasn't much of a cook, he always insisted on having lots of produce and lean protein in his fridge. Perhaps his residency really does keep him extra busy. Or maybe he mostly eats at work.

I rummage through his cupboards before finding a box of Cheerios and pour myself a bowl. (Yes, that means that all I've eaten today is puffed flavored rice or whatever cereal is made of—don't judge me. I'll go for a run tomorrow. Or something.)

I eat it dry because there's no way I'm touching that milk. A girl's got to have some standards.

Once I'm done, I clean the bowl and spoon, grab a water bottle from the fridge, and head back to the living room, where Kevin's still completely conked. I find a notepad and pen and scribble him a note letting him know I'm here if he needs anything. After I place it on the coffee table, I head down the hall.

Where I promptly realize that Kevin has turned his guest room into an office.

Why would he do that?

Whatever the reason, it means I have to either sleep in the recliner—which, as comfortable as it is for movie watching, would be a dreadful place to curl up for an entire night—or in Kevin's bed.

I push open the door to his bedroom and flip on the light. His king-sized bed is covered in a muted gray, goose-down comforter and several pillows, both decorative and regular. In here, Kevin's smell is even more present and I nearly slam the door and retreat.

You've got this, Lola. It's just one night. And Kevin isn't even in here.

Right. I can watch TV on my phone until I fall asleep, then hopefully vacate the premises in the morning before Kevin even knows I stayed in his room.

With that in mind, I head to the en-suite bathroom. I

forego a shower, but wash my face and use some of Kevin's toothpaste to brush my teeth with my finger. Once I'm done using the restroom, I step back into Kevin's room and consider what to do about my clothes. This blouse, while adorable, won't make for a very nice night of sleep. The material will wrinkle and tug and I'll have to lie super still for it to be any version of comfortable.

My eyes flit to Kevin's closet. No, I couldn't …

"You're just being practical, Lola." Aaaaand now I'm talking out loud to myself. Shaking free of the swoony thoughts filling my nostalgic brain, I walk to the closet and find one of Kevin's oldest, most worn T-shirts—one from his high school track days. It's dark blue and will hit just about mid-thigh on me. Perfect for sleeping. Exactly what I need.

Practical. Yep, just being practical.

Steeling myself, I remove my clothing and slip on his shirt.

And darn it if it doesn't feel like coming home.

Groaning like the pitiful sap I am, I grab my phone and pull back the comforter before climbing into Kevin's bed. The crisp percale sheets are cool against my arms and bare legs. I push aside the decorative pillows and tuck a regular one under my head before settling into the softest mattress I've ever known.

I always wondered what it would be like to sleep in this room if Kevin and I got married. Though lots of couples would have slept together after five months of dating (and no judgment for those who do!), we never did. I grew up in a traditional family and wanted to wait until marriage, and Kevin respected that.

But there's something gut-wrenching about being here now, at last—and alone. Single. In Kevin's life, but just for a flash in the pan.

As I bury my face in the pillow of the man I used to love and inhale his scent so it floods my senses, I can't help but wonder if Theresa was right.

Maybe I really am broken.

Because no normal woman tortures herself like this on purpose.

four

. . .

I AM warm and whole and nestled in a cloud of softness.

The air is still around me and a peace I can't explain hums in my chest. Sighing, I turn and snuggle into my pillow—and I bump against something.

No. Someone. A man.

He's warm and smells divine. My fingers fall against the broad planes of his bare chest. I flatten a palm and feel his steady heart pumping blood faster, faster, faster.

I'm dreaming … and it's the best kind of dream.

Since I'm still asleep and will inevitably wake up to an empty bed, I'm going to enjoy myself while this lasts. I snuggle against him and wrap my arm around his torso. In response, he sighs a sleepy assent as his strong arm comes around me. The shirt at my back bunches in his fist.

I thought I might have woken him, but he's still asleep, so I let myself rest in this dream. Mmm. The room is too dark to see his exact features, but it's all right if I never know the identity of Dream Man. After all, it would be kind of disturbing if I knew him in real life. What if his face matches that of the lanky teenager at the grocery store I frequent or my creepy neighbor? I'd have to change stores *and* apartments.

That's the trouble with Real Men—they never live up to the hype of Dream Men. But Dream Men can't disappoint you.

So, before Dream Man can wake up too much, I get even braver (even dreams take bravery, people!) and lift my lips to press a light kiss to the bottom of his jaw.

Dream Man groans with pleasure. "Is this real?"

Crap. I know that voice. And it does indeed haunt my dreams. "Kevin?" I push away from him and sit up.

The movement feels too … real. Like I'm actually awake.

The memory of last night floods back. How Connor left me alone at Kevin's apartment to be here in case Kevin needed me. How I slept in Kevin's bed. In his shirt.

But nowhere in my memory did Kevin come and sleep in his bed too.

And yet … here he is.

"Buttercup?" His voice is drowsy and confused. "What are you doing here?" Now he's sitting up also, and the light cracking through the blinds shows his normally styled hair sticking up at odd angles. It's freaking adorable is what it is, and my fingers itch to push their way through his locks. Itch to—

Nope, nope, nope.

I leap from the bed and hurry to the wall switch, then flood the room with light.

Kevin lifts a hand and blinks against the sudden brilliance for several moments, grunting. Oh, right. Bright light and his concussion probably don't mix. But being in the dark is no good for either one of us.

Of course, seeing things in the light of day isn't so fantabulous either because his bare torso is like a beacon to me. Is it possible that his abs have become even more defined than when we dated?

Get a grip, girl.

Right. I back up and place my hands behind me, anchoring them against the wall.

Like mine, Kevin's breaths come in spurts. That was close. Too close. I almost gave into the dream.

Deep down, did I know it was him? That it was real? And if so, what does that say about me … that I would run back to a man who dumped me so callously? Like a mouse living off crumbs of affection, never knowing if more will be dropped on the ground.

It's pathetic, that's what.

Thankfully, it's morning now. Connor should be here soon. In fact, yes, I think I smell bacon and coffee wafting under the door like the godsend it is. We can finally tell Kevin the truth, and this dream—make that *nightmare*—will be over.

I fidget and realize Kevin is staring at me, his mouth slightly agape. "What?"

He clears his throat and points at me. "You're wearing my shirt."

"Oh. Yeah. Sorry." I tug the hem down—as if that

will cover more of my thighs—and duck my head. "I was just borrowing it."

"I don't mind." Lowering himself to the floor, he walks toward me. His voice is all low and growly, and I am fairly confident it's not because he just woke up. "In fact, I find it just about the sexiest thing in the world."

Oh, sweet Moses. "Uh, why did you come in here last night?"

"This *is* my room. Why did *you* come in here?" His lips curl as he approaches, slow, like a panther stalking its prey.

Is it bad that I've never wanted to be caught more in my life? Probably.

"Y-you fell asleep on the couch and there was nowhere else for me to sleep. I left you a note—"

"I didn't see it." He's nearly to me. If I have any hope of surviving this encounter, of living another day, I've got to get out of here.

"Oh man, do you smell that? It seems breakfast is ready." Then I throw open the door and slip into the hallway, Kevin chuckling behind me.

It's only when I finally reach the kitchen, where Connor is at the stove and all dressed for work, that I realize I'm still wearing Kevin's T-shirt. Before I can pivot and head back to change, Connor turns.

He takes one look at me—and Kevin, who emerges shirtless beside me—and whistles. "Fun night?"

"Shut up." I glare at him and waltz to the coffee pot. There's a rack of mugs—all white and utilitarian—and I snag one.

"You're mean in the morning," Connor teases.

"Only before she's had her coffee." Kevin's voice drifts toward me, and there's something so loving and tender in it, like he doesn't mind that I require caffeine to be a decent human.

And then he comes up behind me, hands at my waist, and nuzzles my neck with his nose. "Don't worry," he whispers. "It's adorable."

I can't take this anymore. Can't do this whole reenactment of the past. Because as much as Kevin believes it is, it's *not* the past.

And he's got to know it.

"You have amnesia!" The words are out of my mouth before I can fully process them. I glance over at Connor and wince.

Connor curses under his breath and pulls the eggs off the burner. The pan clatters against the stovetop.

Behind me, Kevin's body stiffens. I feel the void of him as he steps back. "What?"

I turn a one-eighty and rub the tip of my nose. "When you fell … you forgot the last two years."

He snorts, a strange look on his face, like he doesn't understand me. "Buttercup, you sure have a good sense of humor."

"I'm not joking."

"Wait, what?" Kevin's brow furrows and it takes everything I have not to step into his arms, to reassure him that it's all going to be okay. He turns his attention to Connor. "Is she serious?"

Connor nods. "Afraid so."

Feeling his way backward, Kevin plops into a wooden kitchen chair and shakes his head. "That's not possible." He sits there for several long seconds, hands propped together over his lips like he praying. After what seems like five minutes, he speaks again. "Walk me through this. Why wouldn't the doctors have said anything to me? I'm the patient."

"That was my doing." Connor slides into the seat next to him and Kevin swings his chair around.

I pivot back to face the counter. My thumb moves along the rim of an empty mug while Connor explains the basics of the doctor's report, and I busy myself with pouring three cups of coffee. Outside the window, the sun is still waking up the world, but dark clouds dot the horizon. Looks like it could storm even though we rarely get rain in September. Regardless, birds chirp in the tree just on the other side of the glass, a reminder that maybe there's hope even in the storm.

If nothing else, perhaps after this is over and he gets his memories back, Kevin will be open to talking about what went wrong between us. If I even want that. Do I? Maybe not. Maybe just seeing the old Kevin for a little while will give me the strength to finally forgive him for dumping me with a lame excuse.

Maybe I can finally move on. I thought I had, but being here, feeling the things I am, is proof that Theresa was right. Score another point for the big sister.

I bring two mugs to the table and place them in front of Kevin and Connor, then go back for my own. While Connor continues to review the doctor's findings with Kevin, I dish up three plates of bacon and scrambled eggs, along with some salsa for Kev, just the way he likes it.

When I finally bring everything to the table and take a seat, Kevin turns his eyes on me. "I'm so sorry about all of this." Then, before I can assure him it's fine, his gaze narrows in on my hand—my left hand, to be exact. "Wait." His eyes widen and he looks around the kitchen like he's searching for something. Then he pushes away from the table so fast the chair legs scrape against the tile and emit a high-pitched squawk.

"Kev?" I ask. His cheeks are devoid of color, like when he was in the hospital bed. Maybe his head is pounding again. Is he about to faint? "What are you doing?"

Without answering, he rushes into the living room. Connor and I look at each other and both stand to follow.

But he's not throwing up or collapsing or doing any of the things I thought he might be doing. He's just standing there, fingers gripping the ends of his hair as his gaze roams the room rather frantically. Finally, his eyes settle on me once again, and I've never seen such pain there before. It's like equal parts shock and horror. "You don't live here."

I'm not following his line of thinking. "What?"

He points all over. "My apartment looks the same as it did two years ago. If you lived here, you'd have put up more artwork. You'd have painted the walls and insisted on having colorful throw blankets on the couch, and we'd definitely have teal green or bright yellow plates and mugs in the kitchen. But they're white. They're all white."

"You're right." I say it slowly, like I'm talking to a

child. But part of me is still processing all of this—the fact he's thought about what it would be like if I lived with him. And I'm not quite sure what to do with that information. "I don't live here."

"But … why?" He steps toward me, then seems to think better of it. "I mean, if we've been together so long, why aren't we married? Did you say no when I proposed?"

My lips tremble. I look at Connor, but he's like a deer in the headlights—wide eyes, straight mouth. There's no help coming from that direction. I'm on my own.

I'll try to be as gentle as I can because of Kevin's mental state, but some part of me wants to shake him for what this is doing to my insides.

Moving toward him, I touch his arm. "You never proposed."

"That's not possible. I … I bought a ring. Why wouldn't I have proposed?"

"You what?" His skin burns my fingers and I pull away. That's the first I've heard of a ring. "When?"

"Just a few weeks ago." He blinks. "I mean, two years and a few weeks ago, I guess. Right before my residency started. Come on, I'll show you." Taking hold of my hand, he pulls me down the hall again, into his bedroom, and toward the bureau in his closet.

With a clatter, Kevin tugs open the top drawer and feels all around, flinging neatly folded boxers and socks to the ground in his frenzy. When the drawer is empty, he turns wide eyes on me again. "It's not here. Why isn't it here?" Then he proceeds to search the rest of his drawers one by one, slower, more methodically, as if that will give him the answer he's seeking.

All the while, I'm standing there, bereft. He bought me a ring? And then dumped me a few months later? Why? I don't understand what changed. Well, I do. That conversation we had, after he found the NYU brochure.

After that, things shifted. Even though it had only been five months, I thought our love was strong enough to survive anything.

Apparently he disagreed. Or he'd never really loved me in the first place.

But he bought me a ring.

And that means something. I can't pretend it doesn't.

"Kevin." My voice cuts the air.

He's crouched and rummaging through the final drawer, his eyes narrowed. "It has to be here."

"You must have returned it."

"I know it was early in our relationship, but I just knew, Lola. I knew you were the one for me, so I was impulsive like I never am and I bought a ring. I was going to wait a bit to give it to you." He settles back on his heels, blinking at the last empty drawer. "Maybe on our six-month anniversary. Maybe longer. I don't know when. But I should have given it to you by *now*. It doesn't make sense."

I suck a breath between my teeth. What am I supposed to say to that? Seeing his reaction now is all kinds of confusing. I don't know which way is up and which way is down.

Just rip off the Band-Aid, Lola. "Kevin, we … we aren't together anymore."

Shaking his head, he refuses to look at me. "No. That can't be right."

"It is."

"Why?"

And oh my gosh, I'm about to cry at the anguish in his voice. At the squeezing in my lungs. I snatch my clothes from the spot I left them on his floor last night and run to the bathroom. Flicking on the fan, I bury my face into a towel and scream.

Theresa was right. I never should have come here. Should have let Connor handle this on his own.

There's a knock on the door. "Lola, please. Let me in. Talk to me."

I run the water so I can't hear him. "I just need a minute, okay?"

He mumbles something but the knocking stops. My shoulders relax and I splash my face, slowly pulling myself together. I shed his T-shirt and kick it into a corner like it's on fire. Then I shimmy into my blouse and skirt, run my fingers under my mascara-smudged eyes, turn my head upside down to fluff my hair, and walk out of the bathroom, my legs only slightly trembling.

The bedroom is empty. Just as well. I snag my phone from the bedside table and leave the room.

Connor is sitting on the arm of the living room couch, alone, and he looks up at me. "Hey."

I cut right to the chase as I gather up my purse and slip on my shoes. "I can't help you anymore, Connor."

"I know." A sigh. "That was brutal. But thank you for your help." He glances over his shoulder. "Kev is in the kitchen waiting for us, but go. The doctors and I will handle this from here."

"Okay." I don't trust myself not to burst into tears if I give him a hug, so I just shoot him a final nod instead. "Take care of yourself, all right? And … him."

"I will." A pause. "Lola?"

"Yeah?"

"I don't know what happened between the two of you, but my brother was an idiot to let you go."

A single tear leaks out from my eye. "Bye, Connor." Then, before I can change my mind, I open the door to the apartment hallway and race to freedom.

Freedom from Kevin.

But the memories? I have a feeling those will haunt me for a long time to come.

five

. . .

I'M GETTING WHOOPED by a five-year-old at Monopoly Junior. And, unlike many kids, Sami's not even cheating.

She taps her pert little nose as she considers her next move. It's not like there are a lot of options, but she's still a smart little thing like both of her parents. And with her blonde curls and petite stature, she's basically a mini me of Theresa at the age of five.

It's been eight days since I saw Kevin—but who's counting?—and I've been working at the diner and doing lots of costume fittings for *The Music Man*. But now it's Saturday afternoon and I'm spending a little quality time with the best niece in the world. Okay, the best five-year-old niece in the world. Zoe is only ten days old but already she's stolen my heart too.

Sami passes Go and reaches out her little hand for a payment. "Read 'em and weep," she exclaims. She obviously doesn't know that you only say that in poker, but I'm not going to be the one to tell her.

I just smile and slip her two dollars. "You're good at this game."

She gives an adorable little shrug. "Dad says I'm a natural." There's no pride in her voice—just fact. And I admire her ability to know her own worth without question.

"Don't ever change, Squirt."

Her nose crinkles as she looks at me. "Why would I?"

Again with the confidence. Gah. I love this kid. "Want more popcorn?" I stand and grab our empty bowls.

"No, thanks. I'm gorged."

Laughing at her big word (that's what you get when you have two really smart parents!), I take the bowls to the sink when there's a knock on my door. Glancing at the clock, I frown. "That can't be your dad. He's not supposed to be here for another few hours."

I am of the generation that prefers to pretend they aren't at home when someone unexpected arrives at the door, so I sink back into my chair, determined to ignore whoever is there. But when the knocking persists and I hear a "Lola, I need to talk to you," my hand freezes over my playing piece.

Why is Kevin at my door?

Sami looks at me. "Aren't you going to get the door, Auntie Lo? Mama says it's rude to not answer it." She hops up. "Do you want me to get it?"

"No, sweetie." *Guess I'll be a big girl.* "I've got it." Standing once again, I straighten to my full height, walk to the door, and open it.

"Hey." The look on his face is guarded and unsure, which is so very un-Kevin-like. He's got his hands shoved into the pockets of his navy blue University of San Diego sweatshirt. The weather took a bit of a turn this week for the colder—fall is fully here and I'm not sad about it. But I remember this sweatshirt. I purchased it for his birthday while we were together. "Sorry for showing up like this. I just … there's some stuff I'd like to ask you about, if you have time."

I can't tell by looking at him if he's gotten his memory back. But if he does, then what could he possibly have to ask me? He'd know everything there was to know.

I glance back at the kitchen table, where Sami is counting her money like an adorable little miser. Then I face him again. "I'm kind of busy at the moment."

"Oh." His cheeks blanch. "Do you have … company? I didn't mean to interrupt." He honestly looks like he might hurl.

Does he think that I have a man over here? I should rejoice at his discomfort, but I don't like the idea of inflicting more pain on him. "My niece is here."

His shoulders fall and he huffs out a breath. "I can come back later."

Biting my lip, I study him. "No, it's fine. How about we go to the park down the street? We can talk while Sami plays."

"That would be great."

With a nod, I open the door wider and he steps inside. "Whoa! That can't be Sammy Bear I see over there, can it?"

Sami tilts her head. "Who are you?"

"I'm a friend of your aunt. Kevin."

My heart squeezes, because Sami was only three when Kevin and I dated and she might not remember him—but I remember every second they were together. Every time he lifted her into his arms and cooed her nickname, one of my eggs exploded. Kid you not. I've never wanted to make babies with a man more before in my life.

But that was then. This is now. Their adorable interactions will have no effect on me whatsoever.

My inner self laughs at me and calls me a liar, and she's proven correct when Sami cautiously approaches Kevin and he bends down on one knee and shakes her hand.

Pop! Dang it. There goes another egg.

"So!" I yell much louder than necessary. Both of them startle and glance up at me. "How about a little park time?"

"Yes!" Sami pumps her fist in the air and rushes to the couch for her jacket, which she swoops on in two seconds flat. Before I can say any more, she slips on her shoes and rushes down the hall to use the bathroom.

I take my time getting on my own shoes and jacket—a bright pair of Keds since we'll be walking and a bedazzled jean jacket I found on sale a few weeks ago.

Meanwhile, Kevin walks around my living room examining the various pieces of artwork adorning my walls. I've amassed quite the collection over the years. Each one is unique and yet they're similar too—strokes of color that remind me of the vibrancy of life. Of resiliency. Of who I want to be.

Once Sami returns, we're out the door and headed down the stairs. The air is crisp on our cheeks, but the sun follows through, making it the perfect day to be outside. We walk down the sidewalk to the little neighborhood park up the road, Sami telling Kevin all about kindergarten and how she is learning to read big words and how Tommy Wakefield smells like mustard but that's okay because she doesn't mind mustard even if Jessica Parker says it's yucky.

Kevin smiles and asks her questions back, and *pop pop pop*, it's like a freaking fireworks show in my ovaries. Darn him. I wasn't supposed to have to deal with this anymore after last week.

What could he possibly have to talk about?

At long last (in reality it only took five minutes, but my insides are literally on fire, okay?), we reach the park. There are several kids already having a blast on the three-story play structure and Sami rushes off to join them. Miraculously, I locate an available stone bench nearby and hurry to snag it before someone else can.

Kevin follows, suddenly quiet again.

We both sit and the silence continues between us for a time while we watch the kids play. Their happy laughter is a balm to the zipping static jumping between us, and I close my eyes for the briefest of moments to enjoy it.

Then Kevin clears his throat and the joy slips away.

I open my eyes, find Sami again, and return his ahem with one of my own. "So."

"So." From the corner of my eye, I see Kevin's knee bouncing like a kid on a trampoline. "In case you were wondering, I still don't have my memory back."

That confirms what I already suspected. "I'm sorry." I glance up at him, frowning. "That must be really hard."

"You have no idea." His eyes search mine. "Thankfully, all my physical symptoms are gone. The sensitivity to light, the headaches. I've seen my doctors and they've run even more extensive tests. All of them came back clear."

"That's good, isn't it?" I lift my eyebrows before looking for Sami again. One can never be too careful when kids are playing at a playground and there are a lot of people around, and I won't let Kevin distract me from being a vigilant caretaker.

"Yeah, of course. But it's also frustrating. If there was something on one of the tests, we could fix it. As it is, I just have to … wait."

"Wait for what?"

"For my memory to come back on its own. And … there's no guarantee it will."

Wow. For someone who likes control as much as he does, this has to be killing Kevin. "So what does that mean for your job? Can you go back to work?" Being a doctor is everything to Kevin—and I do mean everything. If he can't do that …

A cloud moves over us, shadowing our bench and bringing with it an extra chill in the air.

He heaves a sigh. "My boss is being really understanding about the whole thing, especially since the accident happened while I was at work. But I can't afford to fall too far behind in my program. They want me to give it a bit more time. See if anything in my memory shakes loose. So for now, I'm just sitting at home twiddling my thumbs."

"That must be torture for you." The edges of my lips twitch with a smile.

"It leaves me a lot of time to think. I've gone round and round in my head and still can't make sense of something. So I finally decided to just … ask."

Ah. I know what's coming before he even has to say it—because that's how things were between us. Despite our differences, we just seemed to understand each other. "You want to know what happened between us."

"Yeah." The word is breathless, filled with an exquisite longing and defeat and relief. So much emotion for one word, but that's the way of it.

Sami is on the swings next to a mom and her son who live in the same building as I do. We're friendly and I trust her. Janine waves at me and I wave back. For the moment, I can take my eyes off Sami and focus on Kevin.

Inhaling, I do.

He straightens at my perusal.

"So you remember starting your residency, right?"

Kevin nods. "I remember about one week of it."

"Well, you might not remember how it was difficult to find time together."

"No, but we knew that was coming. We'd prepared for it."

He's right. We talked through the challenges of being together through his residency, decided to try to eat dinner together a few times a week and sneak in as many texts and phone calls as we could.

"We did. But …" I swallow at the memory. "You were a lot more exhausted than you'd counted on. Your shifts lasted longer than they were supposed to, and you had to cancel on me multiple times. Which was fine. I understood. You were living your dream." I try not to let that last part sound bitter. "But you started to feel like you were falling behind. A lot of your colleagues weren't in relationships at all, and you told me a few times that it was easier for them because they didn't have someone sucking up their rest time at home."

The words sting even now, and forcing them through my lips physically hurts.

Kevin's jaw goes slack. "I said that to you? Wow. I'm so sorry. I sound like such a jerk."

I don't disagree, but his apology does help warm me toward him. "You were mentally and emotionally exhausted. I tried not to let it get to me when you were a bit short."

His hand covers mine on the bench and my heart skitters at the contact.

"I guess I can't blame you for breaking up with me, then."

Inhale. Moment of truth. "Kevin, I didn't break up with you. You broke up with me."

"I wouldn't do that. I love you."

Sweet Moses. I am not prepared to hear those words —ones he's never spoken out loud till now. "Loved me, you mean." And maybe not really.

Kevin winces. "Maybe, but I still feel it so power-fully. Like, it's all I think about, Lola. My world isn't right without you in it."

Oh my stars, he needs to stop saying things like that. "You just think that because you don't remember."

His thumb moves slowly over my knuckles, and the whole park is drowned out by the whoosh of blood in my ears. "I'd think my heart would know even if my brain doesn't," Kevin whispers. "And my heart is telling me things aren't over between us."

Each word is a knife to my self-preservation. I extri-cate my hand, reclaiming it as my own. "But they are. You ended things as if we never meant anything to you at all." My voice trembles. "And you wouldn't even tell me why, but I know."

"Well, I don't." Frustration tinges his words and he stands, pacing in front of the bench. "So please, will you just end my misery and tell me?"

I don't want him lording over me, so I rise too. We face off, nearly nose to nose, his eyes half pleading, half desire, like he's about to kiss me. Over my dead body. Not again, buddy. I give him a little shove in the chest, but like the freaking brick building he is, he doesn't budge.

Fine. He wants to know what happened? I'll tell him.

"We were hanging out in my apartment one night and you found an NYU brochure on my desk."

"NYU? You want to go to NYU?"

I scoff. "That's what you asked that night. I said I didn't know for sure if I was going to apply, but had thought about it for a long while. Then you asked me if I would seriously move across the country when my family was here … when *you* were here."

"Well, that does seem like a valid question, given that I'd just bought you a ring."

"Well"—I emphasize the word sarcastically—"I didn't know that, did I?" Tugging on the ends of my hair, I hold back the desire to stomp my foot. We're probably already drawing attention from all the parents on the playground, but who cares at this point?

Still, I don't want Sami overhearing and reporting back my childish behavior to her parents. So I stretch my neck, close my eyes, and blow out a steady breath before looking up at Kevin again.

"I said I didn't know what I was going to do, but would it even be possible for you to transfer residency programs? I was simply musing aloud, wanting to have a conversation about it. You got really quiet, changed the subject, and never brought it up again." If only we'd talked more that night, maybe things would have been different. "After that, you started canceling our dinners and your texts became really distant and infrequent until you dumped me. Said school was keeping you too busy and you needed to focus on that. And when I begged you to reconsider, to explain yourself to me, you said, 'It's not you, it's me.'"

Kevin groans and grimaces. "I didn't."

"Oh, but you did."

"Lola, I—"

"Auntie Lo!" Sami rushes over, grabbing my hand and tugging at me. "Come push me on the swings. Pleeeeeease."

I glance at Kevin, but realize I don't need his permission. As far as I'm concerned, this conversation is over. He's gotten the information he came for, and now he can go.

I don't have any more to give.

"Bye, Kevin." I follow Sami to the swings and push her until my hands are numb. My feet sink into the blanket of sand beneath, and I remind myself that I'm tired of not knowing where I stand. I need solid ground, and the only way I'm going to get that is to stay far, far away from Kevin Bryant.

The sun starts to set and I check my phone. We've been at the park for nearly two hours. Jake will be by to pick Sami up soon, and the little pixie is looking rather tired. Her black shirt and jeans are covered in dust and dirt, so she could really use a bath too. "Time to get you home, Squirt."

She doesn't even protest, which proves how tired she is. But she does glance over in the direction of the bench I shared with Kevin and wave. "Come on, Uncle Kevin! We're leaving."

What the—?

I turn to find Kevin still sitting there. He isn't gone yet? I figured the fact I left him and didn't look his way for over an hour should have told him I didn't want him to wait for me.

But guess it doesn't matter what I want, because Kevin hops up from the bench and follows us, chatting up Sami once again all the way home as if we hadn't just had a nerve-wrecking conversation an hour ago.

When we arrive back at the apartment, he offers to make Sami some dinner while I give her a bath. Because we're running short on time, I agree, and Sami gets the quickest cleaning known to man. Once she's smelling of lemons and sunshine and all toweled off and dressed in Little Mermaid pajamas, Kevin's got a bowl of mac and cheese all made up for her.

The air smells of pasta and burnt water as I sit her at the table with my phone playing an episode of *Paw Patrol*, and gesture for Kevin to follow me to the front door. "Thanks for doing that."

"No problem." Kevin massages the back of his neck. "Lola, I just want to say … I'm really sorry. It's clear that I hurt you with the way I ended things."

I take a step back. An apology is the last thing I expected from him. "It's fine."

"The thing is … it's not. I wasn't supportive of your dreams even though you've always been really supportive of mine." His eyebrows move together into one. "I mean, it's true that being a doctor means a lot to me. But you … I just don't know what happened."

"Me either." I hug my waist because if I don't, I'll either end up hitting him or hugging him—neither of which will do any good.

"So did you ever do it? Did you ever apply to NYU?"

"No."

"Why not?"

I shrug. "I have my reasons." And he doesn't have the right to hear them, to see inside my heart. Not anymore.

Kevin's fists clench at his side and he gets the same look on his face that he always had whenever he started talking about the politics of being a doctor or when playing a board game he really wanted to win. "Then we have some work to do."

"What are you talking about?"

"I know you have no reason to trust me, but will you meet me for dinner tomorrow night?"

"No." The reaction is knee-jerk, I'll admit. "I can't go down that road again, Kevin."

"I don't mean like a date."

Oh. "What do you mean, then?"

"I have something to show you. Or, I will. If at any point you feel uncomfortable, you're welcome to leave."

I don't speak.

He continues. "We can meet somewhere public, okay? I won't try anything funny. I promise." A pause. "Come on, Lo. You know me."

"I thought I did."

His face falls. "I understand." Then he turns and opens my door. "Thanks for answering my questions today."

"Wait." I say the word before I can stop myself, before I listen to the tingle of warning my inner self is sending my way. "Text me the details and I'll try to be there tomorrow. No promises."

"A chance is all I'm asking for."

And a chance is exactly what I'm afraid of. Because that might be all my heart needs to fall back in love with Kevin Bryant.

If I ever fell out of love with him to begin with.

And I'm starting to suspect that I never did.

six

NEVER HAS a beach made me so nervous before.

I grew up here in San Diego, so it's not like I'm afraid of the water or any beach critters that might come out at night. (Although maybe I should be, given my great-aunt Tildy's propensity for telling stories about sand crabs crawling into her clothes whenever she skinny-dips—and yes, I said "dips," not "dipped." As in, present tense.)

But despite the fire Kevin's got going and the fact he's placed a spread of sandwiches, chips, pasta salad, and fruit between us on a worn woven blanket, I'm not sure what I'm doing here.

And that's bringing a perpetual twitch to my eye.

"Thanks again for coming." He hands me a plastic plate and nudges a spoon into my hand.

"I'm always up for a free meal." Trying to smile, I let my gaze wander the rather deserted beach. It's one that's a bit north of town—one Kevin and I used to frequent together. Maybe that's what has my eye twitching. This feels so … familiar.

And yet, it's different.

I'm different. I'm no longer the naive twenty-two-year-old fresh out of college, ready to take on the world and everything in it. Ready to live my dreams and embrace all the color and brilliance life has to offer. Now, I'm still a lover of color, but I'm more selective. I've realized what really matters.

Of course, love was always on that list. But this time with Kevin has reawakened something in me, something I didn't realize I'd buried. It's poking its head out of the coffin on my insides (there's a picture for you!) and asking if it's safe to come out now. And I honestly don't know what to tell it.

Because it's like I have Kevin back. He's sweet and respectful and not at all like the stressed-out shell of a man he became in those final weeks we were together. Yeah, he's still kind of particular—he was here early and the food is all in matching containers and lined up perfectly straight—but I happen to find this quirk of his adorable. Besides, it's a good trait for a doctor to have. No one wants a sloppy surgeon.

Kevin and I are quiet while we dish up our food. The crunch of chips between my teeth fills in the space when the water recedes. Being near the ocean has always calmed me, and I breathe in the dirt and brine. A chill blows up from the shore and fans the flames of the fire. I snuggle down into my pink sweatshirt and finally force myself to look at the man I've mostly avoided talking to since we arrived.

He's sitting with his knees up, hands propped and grasped together, and instead of eating, he's watching me. When he finally has my attention, he straightens a bit. "So, I've spent the last twenty-four hours researching how to become a costume designer on Broadway."

Of all the things I expected him to say, that was definitely not on my radar. A chip falls out of my mouth. "What?"

He nods. "It seems there are multiple paths you could take—everything from applying to the master's program at NYU to becoming a wardrobe assistant on Broadway and working your way up."

"I already know that."

"Oh. Right. I didn't mean to imply that you didn't." In the waning light, I notice the red rimming his eyes. Did he not sleep well last night? Or at all? I know how he gets when he's invested in something—he goes at it really hard, almost to the extreme. Once, he told me that he used to pull multiple all-nighters in a row before an exam.

But why would this subject warrant such attention from him?

Kevin pulls a folder from inside the picnic basket. "All the info I found is in here, including deadlines for applying to NYU and even some job openings." Clearing his throat, he sets the folder between us and looks at the ocean. "You could even move out there now if you found a job. Start getting to know people. That kind of thing."

His words whirl around me, caressing my cheeks

and slapping them at the same time.

I have no idea how to respond. So I fall to my default—teasing. "Sounds like you're trying to get rid of me."

Kevin swings his head so sharply toward me that I wince at the whiplash I imagine he feels. His eyes swim with intensity in the firelight. "That's the last thing in the world I want. But I was completely selfish two years ago. I know I can't make up for what I did, how I treated you, but ..." Frowning, he huffs out a harsh breath. "But I have to try. Even if the thought of you leaving kills me."

But see, that doesn't make sense. I believe him—it would be hard not to, with the sincerity in his gaze and the fact he just grand gestured the crap out of this moment—but it doesn't help me understand how he could go from *this* to deciding he didn't need me in his life not very many weeks later.

I take the folder in my hands and brush my thumbs along the smooth surface. The folder is neon green and is labeled "Lola's Future." If I were a betting woman, I'd wager everything I have that Kevin did not possess this folder beforehand—that he went out and bought it just for this occasion because he knows that the color is more me than anything he had on hand.

And that makes me want to fling the whole thing in the water, crawl across this blanket, and show him exactly how much I've missed us knowing each other.

"So ... what do you think? Are you ready to start reviewing the information now, or would you like to do that on your own?" The end of the sentence trips up his voice just a tad, as if he really despises the second option.

"Kev," I start, but sudden emotion clogs my throat. After taking a drink of water from my HydroFlask, I try again. "This was really sweet, but I can't move to New York."

"Why not?" Kevin's hardly touched his food, and yet he begins popping lids back onto the containers. The man hates to be idle.

"My sister needs me. She … she had a miscarriage not long after we broke up, and it was super difficult." I spear a bite of pear with my fork and place it in my mouth, allowing the sweet juicy flesh to sit on my tongue several seconds longer than necessary. "I was so glad I was here to help her through that, and it made me realize that near family is where I belong."

Kevin is quiet as he clears the food, stacking them neatly inside the picnic basket and then scooting that aside. "I only met Theresa a few times, but she struck me as someone who would support you no matter what you wanted to do."

"Of course she would. She's been sending me job opportunities for the last year—but all of them would take me away from San Diego."

"And that would be hard. But these are your dreams we're talking about. Right?"

I understand why he's asking for clarification. It's possible that when he found that application to NYU in my apartment, it was the first time I'd ever mentioned my childhood dream of designing costumes on Broadway. I'd just been so caught up in him, in our relationship, that I let that be enough. I let his dreams be enough. And I think I could have been happy staying here, being his wife.

But maybe I always would have wrestled with the unfulfilled dreams. Or at least the fact that I had never fully revealed them to the man I loved. Looking back, I was immature in so many ways. And clearly our relationship was too, since I'd never even shared the deepest parts of my story with him.

I nod. "Right. But …" Should I tell him now? What good would it do?

Seeming to sense my hesitation, he stands and offers me his hands. "Let's take a walk, huh?"

"Okay." I let him help me to my feet and then let go of his hands, tucking mine against my chest while we walk to the shore. I kick off my flip-flops. The squish of cold sand between my toes is so satisfying. A breeze blows my hair backward and I pull my sweatshirt hood up, tucking my hair inside.

We walk a little way, the moon lighting the path before us. There's a line separating the wet ground from the dry sand, and I walk where the water's been while Kevin walks on the loose grains that have yet to be touched. We are together, yet separate.

He stops and points out a few constellations, drawing my eyes upward to a sky I never get to see when I'm in the city limits. It fascinates me—this idea that the stars are always there shining brightly, but we can only observe them if we are in the right place to do so.

Life's like that too, isn't it?

Kevin seems to understand the struggle in my silence, because he quiets too. When I finally look up at him, he's closer than I thought he'd be. If both of us just leaned forward …

He's staring intently into my eyes and I can't help but want to tell him all the things I never did. Not because I expect this to go anywhere. We're on borrowed time, till he gets his memory back and remembers he's better off without me.

But for now, in this moment, he's here.

And I want to be present with him too.

I reach for his hand again. It's slightly callused like my own, and I realize that both of us use our hands to make our dreams come true. Maybe there is more that connects us than I thought. "I promised myself a long time ago that I would never abandon someone I love for the sake of my own dreams."

His squeeze encourages me to go on.

"You know my parents are teachers overseas."

He nods.

I proceed to tell him how they went away when I was so young, how they left me with my sister despite my requests to join them. "They told me that I was in good hands, that the native people needed them more than I did. Do you know what that does to a preteen? It's essentially the equivalent of telling her she doesn't matter as much. That what they wanted—the adventure they'd been dreaming about for years—was more important than me."

"Ah, Lo." He lifts a hand and strokes my cheek slowly with his thumb.

The night breeze has nothing on him, because I shiver at his touch. "I thought I'd driven them away with some of my behavior. I was always getting in trouble at school for talking too much and wearing flamboyant clothes that weren't up to the dress code." I make a face. "Also, once I got into a fistfight because some guys were picking on my friend, Drew, who was in a wheelchair. Those dudes didn't know what hit them." I waggle my eyebrows and laugh at the memory.

He chuckles. "That's my girl." Then it's like he realizes what he says, because he wrinkles his nose. "Sorry. In my brain, we're still …"

"I know."

Kevin pushes back a piece of my hair and my hood falls away. His fingers trace the shell of my ear and linger on my lobe. "I can see why you'd want to be different than your parents, to cherish love and relationships. But I don't think you have to give up your dreams in order to have that. Can't you have both?"

"I don't see how. My sister needs me here to physically help her."

"I thought her mother-in-law lived here now."

It's true. Jake's mom moved from Phoenix this last summer when she got tired of the heat and traveling back and forth to see Sami (and Jake and Theresa, of course). But still. "My sister doesn't have any other family nearby. And anyway, life's greatest treasures aren't in the achievement of something or in the completion of some journey. They're in the journey itself—and that is much better when you experience it with people you love."

"Wow." Kevin's Adam's apple bobs, and his thumb draws a line from my lobe down my jaw and to the corner of my mouth. "Not only are you radiantly beautiful and brilliant, but you're generous and kind too. The whole package."

A blush comes over my face, which heats beneath his gaze and his hand as it cups my cheek. Then Kevin moves closer, and I feel the breath of his whisper on my cheek, in my ear before his lips linger over mine.

Waiting for permission.

For reciprocation.

My insides catch flame again, and goodness knows that I want to lean into it. But I know that in the timeline he's living in, it will only be a month before he will feel very differently about me—and I just can't let myself fall like that again. "Kev."

He pulls back, brow furrowed. "Sorry. I didn't …" And then he's no longer touching me, but instead his hand scrubs his chin. "Just let me say this, Lo. I love that you want to take care of everyone else. I really do. And once upon a time, I guess I was selfish enough to be okay with you giving up everything you wanted for me. But it's *not* okay. You need to follow your dreams. The people who love you will always want that for you."

"I know, but …" My lips tremble. "I don't want to be like my parents. Like …"

"Like me."

I squeeze my eyes shut and don't answer.

"You were always much better than all of us, Buttercup. Don't let what I did dim your light. I would never forgive myself."

I feel his loss the moment he moves away from me. And when I finally open my eyes, he's back at the site of our picnic, putting out the fire in the sand.

Our time tonight has ended. Maybe our time together forever.

But there's an energy buzzing beneath the surface of my skin—and it's got me hoping like nothing has in a long time. I can't even put my finger on what it is, but I know it has everything to do with the man who just spoke truth to my soul. Who encouraged me to follow my dreams.

To leave—even if it killed him.

seven

· · ·

TODAY, not even the smell of greasy fried fish or the scrape of forks against plates or the boring black uniform I'm wearing can upset me.

In my mind, I'm not delivering a hoagie and spare ribs to an elderly couple at Dom's Diner—I'm miles away backstage at Jenkins Theatre, tucked away in my tiny office where I've spent the last week designing.

When I'm creating, everything else falls away. It's just me and the pencil and the paper and the fabric. I also love the transformative stage that takes a costume from concept to reality—the finding, the assembling, the sewing—but that initial stage of discovery is just so magical.

It's also a wonderful distraction from ex-boyfriends who breeze back into your life and attempt to take over your thoughts.

Not that I'd know anything about that. Ahem.

"Hope you two enjoy," I say before heading back toward the kitchen.

"Ms. Flanagan!"

I startle and see Dom advancing toward me from the kitchen, flashing his gold-tooth smile at diners as he passes by. Only late Friday lunchers are here at the moment, and my feet still ache from all the running around I did during the height of the lunch rush.

So much for nothing spoiling my good mood.

I hold back a sigh and force a smile. "What's up, Dom?"

He's a squat little man in his forties who only reaches my shoulders (and I'm not that tall, people—like five-four on a good day), but his presence still holds a whole room captive. Not *captivated*, mind you. He's more like a car accident you can't look away from.

First, he is never seen without a tight white tank under an open button-up that shows off his beer gut and abundance of black curly chest hair. Second, his upper lip is lost in the bushiest dark mustache I've ever seen. Half the staff takes bets on what will be stuck in there next—feta, ketchup, relish. Amy swears she saw an entire spaghetti noodle hanging there once.

But I could look past all of that if the man had any shred of decency. As it is, the only reason I've lasted at Dom's for so long is because Betty, our assistant manager, works around my theater show schedule when she creates the chart each week.

"What's up is that there's a man at table seven who refuses to be served by anyone other than you. What did I say about bringing your boyfriends here?"

"I don't have a boyfriend." I peek over his head to the corner booth, and there's Kevin perusing a menu. I haven't heard from him since our picnic five nights ago, so I definitely didn't expect to see him here now.

My stomach trots like a pony at a show.

"Don't have a boyfriend, huh?" Dom's self-satisfied smirk could win him first prize in a Smug Jerk of the Year contest. "I better not see you slacking or else."

I want to roll my eyes and ask "or else what?," because I'm so much more responsible than most of the high school or college-aged employees here who come into work hungover or make out in the walk-in pantry.

Instead, I fit my lips with a smile and brush past Dom, leaving the strong scent of his sage pomade in my wake. As I approach Kevin's table, my hands fidget with the edge of the black canvas apron I'm wearing.

He looks up when I get close and offers me a tentative wave. "I see that Dom's still as friendly as ever."

A snort leaves my nose and I rush to cover it with a cough, sure that Dom is watching us interact. I lift my notepad and pen from the pocket of the apron and poise the pen over the pad. "Do you want your usual?" Every time Kevin would visit, he had the same thing: a grilled chicken Caesar salad, hold the croutons.

"I was thinking about switching it up."

My hand falters. "You were?"

In the background, the bell jangles over the diner's front door, but I'm riveted to the spot. This is the man who fought me every time I wanted to try a new Thai restaurant or go salsa dancing past his usual bedtime (yes, he had a bedtime, like an old man). I mean, sure, I finally wore him down and got him to hang a colorful piece of art in his living room, but the man is all about his routines.

Or … he was.

At my question, he nods. "Something about forgetting two whole years of your life—and not knowing if you'll ever remember them—makes you wonder if maybe there isn't a reason it's all happening, you know?"

"You mean, it's not all just about the logical consequences of falling and hitting your head, but something bigger?"

He and I used to talk a lot about the mysteries of the universe. While I tend to be more of a mystic, he's a man of science. "Something like that."

Huh. Maybe old dogs can learn new tricks after all.

"So." I tilt my head as I study him more closely. He's clean-shaven again, and his tight blue Henley softens the lines around his pupils, making it appear as if he's looking into my soul instead of merely scrutinizing me. "What would you like?"

"For you to join me."

The pony in my chest increases his pace and now he's cantering back and forth, picking his feet up high and flinging his mane. "Oh. Um." I pause. "But why?"

He places the menu flat on the table and holds up his hands. "Look, I don't have any right to ask you to spend time with me. I know that. But my memory hasn't returned yet, and I feel like there's a piece of me missing. You."

I take a step back and he groans. "Sorry, didn't mean to get all cheesy. The truth is, I had some good news today and I could only think of one person I wanted to share it with. Do you think that you could ever forgive me for what I did? Could we be … friends?"

Friends? With Kevin Bryant, breaker of my heart, the man I thought I might love forever?

I have to be honest. "I don't know." At his nod of understanding—and eyes filled with pain and resignation—I glance back at the clock mounted above the kitchen. "But at the very least, I could take my break and let you tell me your good news."

"I'll take anything you're willing to give me."

My lips quirk. "Does that include food?"

"Sure." He pushes the menu my way. "Surprise me."

I scurry away, not able to contain my grin, and glide through the swinging white door to the kitchen where steam hits me in the face and I nearly choke on the thick scent of burgers frying.

The two other servers who haven't been cut stand near the back of the kitchen flirting with each other. I roll my eyes and turn to the cook, Big Joe—an ironic name if ever I heard one, since the balding man can't weigh more than one hundred and fifty pounds. He grins at me and asks who my feller is.

"Just an old friend." Friend. I try out the word on my tongue and it tastes funny, like those carbonated waters that you expect to be sweet but aren't. "Can you throw on a couple of specials for table seven, please?"

"I've got five orders ahead of ya."

"Please?" I bat my eyes and pucker my lips like Sebastian in *The Little Mermaid* when he's instructing Ariel how to win a man.

Big Joe laughs and waves his spatula at me. "Two specials coming right up."

Leaning in, I give him a kiss on his weathered cheek. "You're the best."

"Aw, shucks. Get on with ya, then."

I shout at Tanya to stop flirting with Nick and then deliver a few platters to one of my tables. By the time Joe's got my plates ready, I've checked in on my two other tables and hung up my apron. "Taking my fifteen!" I yell at no one in particular as I take the plates from Joe and toss a side hip at the swinging door.

When I set Kevin's dish in front of him, his wide eyes make me giggle. I slide into the seat across from him.

"What is this exactly?"

I pick up a silverware setting and unroll the napkin. "Haven't you ever had carne asada fries before?" Of course, I know he hasn't. The man is the picture of health—he's a doctor, after all. But he really needs to learn to live a little, and I always made it my mission when we were together to get him out of his comfort zone. Why should being his friend be any different?

You're lying to yourself, Lola Flanagan. You can never be just friends with this man.

I ignore my inner self and stab a french fry laden with charred steak, guacamole, melted cheese, and pico de gallo. It may seem like a strange dish for a diner, but

Dom added it to the menu after the hundredth or so tourist asked if we made them.

To Kevin's credit, he doesn't curl his lip and refuse to try his fries. In fact, he surprises me when he pulls a dripping fry from the middle of the stack. *"Bon appétit."*

We take bites of our lunch at the same time, and if the groan coming from him is any indication, he's digging the fries. It reminds me of a similar sound he made when I kissed his jaw the other morning in his bed …

Gah! I've tried very hard not to think about that. How safe and secure I felt. How there was nowhere else I wanted to be.

How I wasn't at all disappointed when I learned the identity of my Dream Man.

The pony is galloping now, pounding the rocks encasing my heart into pebbly dust. Its hoofs are slicing at the tender muscle beneath—a reminder that I'm both fragile and strong.

"Good, right?" I manage. Slurping down a sip of cool water, I force myself to continue the conversation as if a thousand inconsistencies aren't dancing through my brain. "What's the good news?"

"I saw my doctor again."

"Oh?"

"Yeah. He's probably getting sick of me, but we're two and a half weeks out from the accident and still no memories from the last two years have returned."

"What did he say about that?"

"To be patient."

"Is that all?"

"No, he also said that something will possibly trigger a flood of memories when I least expect it. It could also be more like a trickle effect, coming one at a time. Or there's the third, worst possible option ..." His shoulders slump and he taps his fork against the laminate tabletop.

I know what he's thinking. "That your memory might not come back at all."

"Yeah. But even though it would be terrible, I thought it would put me two years behind in my training."

For him, that *would* be tragic, since being a surgeon is so important to him.

"But it won't?"

He shakes his head. "Today I also met with my boss and he let me have a go at the robot arm—just to see how I'd do." I remember him telling me about the tool that doctors use to practice and improve their surgical techniques. "And do you know what happened, Lo?" Where he was slightly dejected a minute ago, now he's moved to the edge of his seat, his voice giddy like a kid at an amusement park.

"What?"

"I don't remember actually learning these techniques or ever doing them before, but ... my hands did."

"Really?"

"Yes!" He laughs. "It was so bizarre, and I got into my head about it at first. But when I let my mind go still, then my body took over."

"So is that sort of the equivalent of regaining your memory?"

"Not really, but it should allow me to go back to work soon." He grins and grows even more ruggedly handsome in a split second. "My boss and my doctor both agree that if I can study my butt off and successfully demonstrate a few more techniques next week, they'll fully reinstate me to the program. I won't be delayed much, if at all."

"That's really great news, Kev." And it is. Only …

"What's wrong?"

Biting the inside of my lip, I push my plate of now cold fries away. "Sorry, I don't mean to be a bummer. It's just that …" I exhale. "You work a lot. And last time, you got so focused on succeeding, almost to the detriment of everything else."

He hesitates, then scoots around the booth toward me until our shoulders are touching. "You mean us, don't you?"

I shrug against him and take a beat before saying more. "It's a noble profession, but why does being a doctor mean *that* much to you? Is it because of your mom?" Is he desperate to save everyone else because he couldn't save her from cancer?

His breath hitches and I expect him to pull away, to shut down, to deflect—but he doesn't. "I don't know. Maybe, although I was already in med school when she was diagnosed. But there is part of me that feels like because of that, I should have known something was wrong with her, you know? Maybe I could have convinced her to get tested sooner."

"Kev, even your dad didn't see it, and he lived with her."

"I know that, but—"

Dom's throat clears so loudly I hear it from across the room. How did I completely forget that more than just Kevin and me exist in this moment? Glancing up, I find my boss, who is tapping his watchless wrist at me near the kitchen. It's ridiculous, because there's like one customer in the whole place other than Kevin and Tanya and Nick are both still here.

But you know what? Some things are more important than a job. I hold up my hands, indicating I've got five more minutes.

He just grunts and turns on a heel, vanishing into the kitchen.

Shaking off Dom's bad juju, I soften my voice and glance up at Kevin again. "So what made you go into medicine in the first place? Your dad?" Something is driving the obsession, and I don't think it's just Kevin wanting to be the best.

"That's part of it, I guess." He sighs and picks up my fork, twirling it between his fingers. "There's this moment that has stuck with me ever since I was ten. We were at the beach, and Connor and I were boogie boarding, having a blast until …" A shudder vibrates through him—through me. "Until Connor fell off his and nearly drowned."

"Whoa."

"Yeah." The fork tines poke the black rubber casing that edges the table. "It happened so suddenly and I didn't even notice we were near a riptide. Dad came crashing into the water beside me and pulled him out, then did CPR on the beach." A breath. "It was the scariest moment of my life."

"I can't even imagine." And I can't. I've never been the older sibling, but I've been an aunt, and the thought of something like that happening to Sami … my stomach twists. "So you saw your dad saving your brother's life and wanted to do the same?"

"Yeah."

But the hesitant way he says it indicates that there's more to the story. I could pry, but I'm kind of curious if he will tell me on his own.

And then, miracle of miracles, he does. "I came out of the water, leaning over Connor, wanting to help, and my dad pushed me aside. He said …" Kevin swallows, his face contorted with the pain of the memory. "He said if I hadn't been distracted with my own pleasure—if I'd been paying more attention, been more focused—it never would have happened."

I can't help the gasp that leaves my lips. "But you were just a kid!"

A sad smile strains and pulls against Kevin's mouth. "You've met my dad."

Yeah, I have. And if he was here right now, I'd have some choice words for him. And suddenly, something clicks in my brain. "Kev, is that why you broke up with me?"

"I don't remember breaking up with you, so how can I know?" He doesn't ask in a mean way, just a confused one.

"Well." I gently remove the fork from him and slip my

palm into his. Then I lean back a bit so we are sitting side-ways on the booth, face to face. "I know you want your life to mean something. You want to help people. It's who you are. But maybe you've also told yourself that the only way to make that happen is by depriving yourself. By creating a plan and sticking with it. Your plan was med school and a six-year residency at USD. That was the perfect way to honor your parents and save people and give your life purpose. But then I came along and—"

"And I realized that being with *you* gives my life purpose."

I give him a sad smile. "I was going to say that I wrecked all of your plans."

"That's not the way I remember it."

"You're the one with amnesia, remember?" Except … there's a part of me that wonders. Wonders if—now that we've shared a bit more, talked through some of this stuff—Kevin has changed his tune.

Maybe there could be something between us again.

If only I have the courage to reach for it and explore.

"Kev—"

And it's just like Dom to break the magic of our moment when he stomps over, places his hands on the table, and says in the most menacing voice he can muster, "Your break is over, Ms. Flanagan. You'll have to make eyes at each other on your own time." Then he spins and leaves.

I groan. "Sorry about him."

"No problem." A pause. "Hey, Lo?"

"Yeah?"

"Thanks for this."

"You're welcome."

"And … well, you asked me why I wanted to become a doctor. Someday I'd like to hear more about why you love costume design."

I smile, a sudden idea forming. "Maybe I'll just have to show you."

eight

I AM one thousand percent in my element here.

Flipping on the light, I inhale my favorite scent in the world—clothing. Some thrift stores smell musty, but inside the theater's tiny costume room, it's more like softened dirt after the rain. A vintage tinge of use hangs in the air, like at the old stacks inside a university library.

Only here, instead of books, it's fabric that's telling a story.

"You made all of these?" Kevin steps toward a tall rack with several early-1900s day dresses.

I know he's wearing a simple gray T-shirt and jeans, but my eyes follow him like I'm in a desert and he's a freaking oasis. Dang, the man is fine. He fits in perfectly with the works of art surrounding us.

When he lifts his eyebrows at me, waiting for me to answer, I snap out of my internal analogies and scurry to join him. "Yes and no." Pulling at the skirt of one of the outfits so it remains on the hanger but gives us a view of the whole dress, I thumb the light linen material. "For some, I started with a base dress and added embellishments or sewed on extra fabric. For others, I found a pattern from 1912 and went to town sewing the whole thing myself."

"That's awesome." He shakes his head, gesturing around the room. "I could never do something like this. I'm not creative enough."

From the stage area, the muffled sound of music makes its way to us. Rehearsal has begun, but as I don't have any fittings scheduled and this isn't a dress rehearsal tonight, we should be left alone.

"And I could never operate on someone." I smile teasingly. "The world needs all types." Dropping the skirt, I move to my main work area—a large desk that's littered with paper drawings, buttons, bits of ribbon, a few pincushions, thread, and scissors—and pick up a large woman's hat with a festoon of feathers. "I've especially enjoyed the hat wear in this show. It's so fun."

"All the colors, the fabrics—they're really you. I can see why you like it." He walks toward me and picks up a sailor's straw hat used for one of the men in the show's barbershop quartet. "Though it's a little bit like a cave in here. How do you work like this?"

"I think it's cozy." He's right, in a way—the ceilings are low and saggy, the canned fluorescents the only source of light since this costume room is in the basement of the theater. In the winter, it gets chilly thanks to the concrete floors and a temperamental heater that only likes to work some of the time. "I can spend eight or ten hours straight in perfect solitude down here—nothing but me and my fabrics."

"Well, I can't wait to see the show. I'm sure it's going to be as amazing as its designer."

My heart hangs onto the fact he wants to come to see the show. He never made it to *Beauty & the Beast*—we broke up the weekend before its run. But *The Music Man* performance isn't for another three weeks. Does that mean he's planning to still be in my life?

Take it easy, Lola. Don't get ahead of yourself.

My inner self is, once again, right.

"Thanks for the compliment." I take the hat from Kevin's hands and plop it onto his head, tilting my own to study him with a smile. He looks amazing. Like this garb that's over a hundred years old, Kevin's good looks are timeless. "But I ultimately have to remember that my job isn't just to make visually stunning pieces. It's to make an actor feel like his character. To help him bring that character to life."

"How do you do that?" Kevin stares down at me, but the brim of the hat shadows his eyes a bit, making it hard to interpret them.

I shrug. "The details. Those are what make a costume come alive. It's not just the type of fabric, whether it's dingy or bright, or the colors. It's finding the perfect hat to go with the cloche, the detailing on the buttons even if no one in the crowd can see them from far away. It's creating clothing that doesn't quite fit if the character is someone who would be too cheap or too embarrassed to buy a new shirt after gaining weight. It's …" I scrunch up my nose, trying to explain. "It's not just about the effect. It's about letting the clothes stand for something."

He removes the hat from his head, dusts it off, and sets it gingerly back onto my desk. "I love the idea, but I'm a black and white kind of guy."

I drop my jaw in pretend shock. "Not you."

"Ha ha." He playfully pokes me in the side, right where he knows I'm ticklish. Before he can get me again, I dodge him. "Help a guy out, Buttercup. I need an example."

Laughing, I snag Kevin's hand, drag him to a separate rack in the back corner of the room, and start searching. As I move hangers, their scrape against metal fills the air. Finally, I locate one, two, three dresses and hang them facing outward on the rack. The first is a no-nonsense brown dress with a stiff skirt and collared shirt made of sturdy fabric. Next is a simple daydream with a smattering of yellow and a bit more softness to it. The last one is pink with bows and a full skirt.

"Okay, take Marian Paroo, the main character in this show. This might be something only I notice, but the progression from one dress to the next represents her character arc in the show." I run my finger along the swooping neckline of the third dress. "She goes from stiff and unrelenting to softened by love."

I'm mesmerized by the silky feel of the material under my fingertips. By the stillness of the moment.

But when Kevin speaks, it's anything but an intrusion. "I get it now." His voice is husky. And even though it's just a whisper, it reverberates in my soul. "It's really something. *You're* really something."

Whew. I shake loose of the spell that the costumes have cast over me and push them to the side. Then, in an attempt to break apart some of the intensity of the moment, I turn and grab hold of the empty clothing rack bar hovering above me, gripping it like a gymnast about to do a routine. "Maybe I just like the theatrics." I toss my head back and make a mock-serious face. "The drama."

He chuckles, and it is full and deep and filled with joy. It's honestly the most beautiful sound in the world.

"You should do that more often, you know," I say.

"What?"

"Laugh." I bite the inside of my cheek. "You're so serious most of the time. Don't they say laughter is the best medicine?"

He takes a step toward me, amusement in his eyes. "Who is 'they'?"

"You know. The universal they." I quirk a grin.

"Oh, right." Another step. "Given their distinguished reputation, I should definitely start taking advice from them."

I stick out my tongue at his sarcasm. "Take advice from me, then."

"As you wish."

And darn it if he hasn't taken this teasing moment and turned it serious with three little words—words from our favorite movie.

Words he used to whisper to me right before kissing me senseless.

I stiffen and my hands hold the bar above me even tighter as he continues to advance one slow step at a time. The music onstage has picked up speed, a moving, rolling dance, but I'm pinned to the spot. My brain is no longer functioning—and I might just be okay with that. I'm stuck in this in-between moment, where the reality of what has been is about to meet the reality that is.

The reality that could be … if only.

Then Kevin's hands skim my waist before he takes the final step and closes the distance between us. My lungs are burning from the fact I'm mostly holding my breath, but to breathe would be to move on to the next moment.

And I'm equally terrified of and exhilarated by it.

He leans in, closer, closer, and kisses my forehead. Then his mouth moves to my temple, down, down, to explore every inch of my ear before taking my neck captive. I can't help the soft moan that releases when he hits that magical spot behind my jaw, and I lean my head to the side to give him better access.

He happily complies with my unspoken request, proving once again that he knows me and I know him despite our long absence from each other.

Shivers lick their way up my spine, igniting every nerve and heating the cave inside my chest. As his lips make their way to the crook of my collarbone, they are just as intense—yet somehow as gentle—as I remember, and my body quivers at this reminder of what I used to have.

One of his hands skates up the center of my back, pressing me even closer to him. It's possessive, claiming me. Or so I think, anyway. But what if I'm wrong?

It might break the magic of the moment, but I have

to know. Because, as foolish as it might be, I've started to allow hope to bloom in that barren field of my heart —hope that maybe, just maybe, there's still a chance for us. But what if, for him, it's just muscle memory?

Don't worry about that now. Just enjoy this.

My mind and my heart are lobbing all the grenades at each other, and I honestly don't know who is going to win. Maybe they'll destroy each other and I'll go crazy.

Maybe I already am, to be considering this.

"What are we doing?" I whisper.

Kevin freezes, his hot lips pressed against my skin, and then he pulls back to look at me. Because my hands are nearly numb from hanging onto the bar above me, I allow them to drop around his neck. My thumbs make little circles in the bottom of his hairline as I wait for his answer.

Finally, he gives me one. "Lo, I absolutely hate that I was so focused on myself two years ago. That I pushed you away when I should have been finding a way for us to be together. That I let go of the best gift the universe ever gave me. And I can't help but think that by erasing the last few years in my mind, fate is giving me a second chance. A chance to be a different man. To choose differently. To choose you."

I have dreamed of this moment many times over the last two years, wondered how I would react if Kevin said what he's saying to me now. Would I push him away? Would I tug him close?

My heart pulls the pin of its final grenade and tosses it at my brain. It explodes, and like a mirror shattering, there are a million tiny refractions of light bringing brilliance to the moment.

I'm done being a soldier on love's battlefield. The fight is over. I toss my figurative gun aside and yank Kevin's lips to mine so forcefully that we topple backward into the rack of clothing.

Crap! We fall to the ground, our descent slowed only by a few costumes that slide off their hangers as we twist and thump. Thankfully, my head is pillowed by the costumes that caught me when we fell.

"Are you all right, Lo?" Kevin's concerned voice is floating above me, but I can't see anything until I sit up and pluck a pair of bloomers off my head. I look at where he's hovering beside me, face contorted with worry—and I laugh. And laugh. I can't help the joy bubbling up from my chest.

That was the last thing in the world I expected to happen, but surprises are what make life worth living. After all, a surprise is how I found Kevin again. How I'm here with him right now, in this hilariously ironic moment, surrounded by two things that make me feel alive.

Costumes I created.

And him.

A smile replaces the confusion on Kevin's face. "Life with you is never boring, is it, Buttercup?"

Before I can come up with a witty reply, he leans over and kisses me sweetly. His lips taste of peach tea—his favorite—and they're warm and firm. When they part and his tongue joins mine, my hands find his T-shirt and hold on for dear life.

Boring? No.

Being with Kevin is the exact opposite. I feel like I'm a haughty trapeze artist walking a tightrope without a net, reveling in the rush of adrenaline and the heat that's crackling through every pore of my being like lightning.

I'm taunting the universe, saying *Bring on the wind and rain. Ain't nothing going to knock me down.*

And when Kevin leans me back into the array of colorful fabrics covering the ground—kissing me all the way—I realize that if I'm going to fall, then this is definitely the way to go.

nine

. . .

"YOU SURE ARE HAPPY TONIGHT."

My sister flashes me a tired smile as she walks into the nursery where I'm rocking baby Zoe. The moonlight in the upstairs room spills in through the gauzy pink curtains. It's pure peace, and I've been taking the opportunity to not only cuddle my niece but relive the last two days with Kevin.

There have been more serious talks.

Some *Princess Bride* watching.

And lots and lots of kissing.

What? We're making up for lost time.

But my sister doesn't need to know that's the reason for my quiet grin, so I deflect. "Who wouldn't be happy while holding this absolute squish?" My newest niece is only two and a half weeks old, but she's already got as many rolls as the Pillsbury Dough Boy—and I love it.

"Uh-huh." Theresa ambles to the white crib in the corner, picks up a fuzzy blanket that's hanging askew, and folds it neatly before draping it over the edge again. "Thing is, I've seen that smile before." She angles a mom look at me—you know the one. Pursed lips, squinty eyes, raised brows.

I pretend not to hear her and trace the edge of Zoe's tiny nose with my fingertip while she sleeps. "Is Sami down for the night? I heard lots of giggles and splashes coming from the bathroom."

"Jake's putting her down now." Theresa crosses her arms over her chest and leans back against the crib rails. "Which gives us alllllll night to talk."

A threat if I ever heard one. "You should really use the fact I'm here to your advantage. Go get some sleep."

"I will—once we've talked."

I roll my eyes up to the ceiling, where the fan slowly stirs the air. Then, groaning, I ask, "What do you want to know?"

"Are you and Kevin back together?" My sister's voice wobbles, causing me to turn my attention back to her. Theresa is all kinds of things—bossy, loving, generous, opinionated, ambitious.

But frightened isn't one of them.

And yet, her question is filled with vulnerability, softness—fear.

"Reese."

She arches an eyebrow, her expression wiped of all but intensity. "Lo."

I sigh. "Yes, we're back together." At least, I think we are. We haven't really defined what we are, but I'd think the fact we spent thirty of the last forty-eight hours together probably speaks to there being something significant between us.

When Theresa scrunches her face and grunts, I shift Zoe in my arms and stand so we're on equal footing. "It's not like last time, okay?"

"And what's changed, exactly? Kevin still thinks it's two years ago, doesn't he? So he doesn't remember what it was like to do his residency and date you at the same time—how stressful that was for him. He doesn't remember dumping you like a hotcake." My sister pats her chest. "But I do. And I don't want that for you again, Lola."

"I know." I bounce my niece while considering how to answer Theresa's question. "You asked what's changed? Me, for one."

With a skeptical look, Theresa takes Zoe from me without asking and, after a sweet kiss to her forehead, places Baby Girl on her back in the crib. Then she juts her chin toward the door and we sneak out together. She leads me to the kitchen, stopping at the fridge to grab us two cans of lime La Croix before unlatching the back door and sliding it open.

I follow her into the evening breeze. Her backyard is small, but a few large trees offer a canopy of leaves over us as we settle into the white wicker chairs on her back patio.

"You're right, Lo. You have changed. You've matured and grown in your own confidence, and the work you're doing is amazing."

The hiss and pop of Theresa's can as she opens it echoes into the night. A neighbor must be grilling, because the smell of sizzling meat wafts from somewhere nearby. Meanwhile, katydids make rasping, punctuated music from some unknown orchestra pit.

"Thanks." I thumb over the letters in the logo on my can.

"But it takes two people to make a relationship work."

"Of course it does. And Kevin is willing to do the work." At least, I think he is. It's not like we've talked that in-depth yet about what all of this means—or even what he sees long-term.

"It's just … what happens if he regains his memories? Don't you think he'll go back to being that super-focused guy who believes his work and his dreams are more important than yours?"

My stomach churns as Theresa voices the question that's gone round and round in my own head. I blurt out the only answer I have that allows me to pretend it's all okay. "He's changed too."

"Has he?"

"Reese, he took me to the beach and spent the entire time outlining paths I could follow to become a Broadway costume designer."

She flicks lightly at the soda pop top. "Really." It's a statement, not a question—and the statement says she doesn't quite believe it.

I tuck a piece of hair behind my ear and nod. "He even brought me an NYU application and a whole folder of current job opportunities."

"Huh." Theresa sits back in her chair and takes a sip of her drink, staring up at the moon playing peekaboo with us from behind the clouds. "So have you applied to any of them?"

"No."

"Why not?"

I'm quiet. I can't tell her that she's part of my why not.

"I just don't understand. You have so much potential—and you were made for more, Lola. You're caging your talent by staying here and working small shows that don't even pay you for your time."

"Volunteering is fun." I try to add conviction to my voice, but it comes out defensive and stiff. Sighing, I try to make her see the truth. "I don't need the accolades or flashy attributes or a bigger stage."

"But the bigger stage needs you."

Her words spark something to life inside of me—some flame that I've snuffed out. But lighting it again will do absolutely no good.

"I—"

"Look at me, Sis."

So I do, and she reaches over to grip my hand. "When you do something you love—when you contribute something beautiful to the world—the whole world is better for it. And not that you can't do that here, but … I don't know. I just hate to see you settling."

"I'm not settling. I'm choosing."

"But are you choosing out of fear?"

Am I? I wouldn't say that, exactly. "I'm choosing what's best."

"Best for who?" She tilts her head. "For you? Or for Kevin? Because forgive me for saying so, but you cannot make your plans around that man. He's already proven that he will make decisions for the both of you—and I don't want that to leave you floundering, without a Plan B. In fact, I don't want you to change your Plan A just to accommodate him."

"I'm not." I gently extricate my hand and place it around my La Croix, which I have yet to even open.

"Just let me ask you this. If you didn't have to choose between him and your dreams, would you go to New York?"

"No." Because there's more to consider—namely, two little nieces and a big sister who need me.

"I don't believe you."

We're quiet for a good while, long enough that I have to look over to see if Theresa is still awake—with as little sleep as she's getting these days, I wouldn't be surprised if she'd conked out.

But she's just sitting there, worrying her lip, staring at the stars that litter the bits of sky seen through the branches. Finally, she speaks. "I don't think I could have survived the last few years without you, Sis."

My hand darts out to grab hers again. I shouldn't have let go in the first place. "Same here."

"But ..." She rubs the bottom knuckle of my fourth finger—right where Kevin's ring would be sitting if things had played out differently a few years ago. "I never meant to trap you here."

My head swings around and my gaze collides with hers, meeting her in the dimming darkness. "What? You didn't."

"I'm not dumb, Lola. You're obviously staying here for a reason." A pause. "Tell me I'm wrong."

I could, but I don't want to lie. "I don't feel trapped at all."

She shakes her head as if I've just said the sky is neon pink or that Jenna Stauffer (a girl who tortured me in junior high) is my bestie. "I'm not stupid, Lo. You were filled with ambition and dreams until a few years ago. So if it's not Kevin, then it's me."

I open my mouth, then close it again.

"See? You can't lie, so you're not saying anything."

"It's not like that, though. I've just realized what's important. And being here for you, for the girls, is the most important thing."

She leans forward and her hand grips mine like she's never letting go. "I love you for saying that, but we are fine. That doesn't mean I don't need you—I always will —but we can still be close even when you're physically far away."

"We've seen that isn't true."

Her nose scrunches for a moment, then her eyes widen and she nods. She squeezes my hand even harder. "We aren't Mom and Dad, Lola. Yes, being long distance makes things harder, but love will always find a way. And I love you up, down, around, and back again, little sister."

There she goes, making my eyes burn again. I scoot closer and lay my head on her shoulder. "To the moon and back."

"Now that that's settled, what's your next move?"

I smile despite myself. "So pushy."

"It's my right as a big sister." She nudges me with an elbow. "So? Should we get started on that application for NYU?"

How will Kevin react if I do that, now that we're back together? Maybe Theresa's right—I should make this decision independent of him, because who knows where we will be next fall?

It couldn't hurt to have a few different options, right? Applying doesn't mean I'll get in. And getting in doesn't mean I have to go.

"Fine. But only if you have coffee."

"Please, I've got two kids." Theresa snorts. "Of course I have coffee."

ten

· · ·

I AM ROSE DEWITT BUKATER, Kevin is Jack Dawson, and our speedboat is the Titanic.

Hmmm. Never mind. As romantic as it sounds, I don't think I like that analogy very well, considering the ending they had. Also, we're not exactly at the front of the boat because have you ever stood there while a boat bounces through the water? Let's just say, water up the nose is less than sexy.

So fine, my entire analogy is falling apart (what's new?), but that doesn't stop me from enjoying my spot behind Kevin as he drives us around the San Diego bay on a lazy Monday afternoon. He's sitting at the wheel and I've got my arms around his neck, alternately taking in the sights and nibbling at his ear.

"You'd better stop doing that if you don't want me to crash."

My laughter is drowned out by the motor rumbling beneath our feet, the drone of planes passing overhead, the call of gulls in their flight to and from the sand. We're close enough to the land to see the sights—from Coronado Island to the USS Midway to the buildings of downtown San Diego—but far enough that we can't make out the outline of people.

It feels like we're the only two people that exist, and I am here for it. It's been about a month since Kevin and I found each other again, and more than two weeks since we finally gave in to the pull of the past. And it's been magical—but also a reminder. Because with Kevin working again, I have started to remember just how busy residency keeps him.

How much harder we have to work just to sneak in time together.

Which is why we're here right now. I surprised him with this boat rental, knowing it was something he and his dad used to do together when he was younger. He always said he felt most like himself when he was out on the water, and after the stress of the last few weeks— filled with work, but no returned memories—I knew he needed a day like today.

We need a day like today.

"So," I say right in his ear to make sure he can hear me. "I shouldn't do this?" My fingers, which are dangling over his chest, fiddle with the top button of his lightweight shirt. When I pop it open, I skim my thumbs along the ridges of his collarbone.

"Lo …" he warns in that delicious growl.

"Or this?" Leaning down, I press a kiss to the vein throbbing in his neck.

"That's it." He lets off the gas and I squeal as he

turns and snags me around the waist. When he pulls me onto his lap and his lips claim mine, I don't resist. We are two beats of the same heart—and that makes what I have to tell him even harder.

Don't think about that right now, Lola.

But though I try, I do not have the happy talent of compartmentalizing my feelings, and Kevin stops kissing me. He pulls back to look into my eyes. "What's wrong?"

I both hate and love that he knows me so well.

Though it's mid-October, the sun is full-on showing off today, warming the skin of my face and bare arms as I loop them around his neck and place my forehead against his. "I don't want to ruin this."

"*This* as in this date, or *this* as in … us?"

I frown. "Both, I guess."

He blinks and kisses me on the nose, sitting back to see me better. "This sounds ominous."

"I don't mean for it to be. It's … well, exciting. But also …" He's right. "Yeah, it feels a bit ominous too, I guess. Exciting and ominous. Oh, I don't know." I pop off his lap and start pacing the boat deck, which isn't very large. There's not really anywhere for me to go, but in this moment, I have to move.

Kevin runs a hand through his hair, showing off his bicep in the process. "I know the last few weeks have been a lot, and I'm sorry."

"It has nothing to do with that."

"Okay." He cocks his head, waits.

Blowing out a breath, I stop to chew my bottom lip. "I got an email last night." A pause. "From NYU."

His eyebrows lift. "NYU? Wait, did you apply or something?"

"I did. A few weeks ago."

"Oh." That one word is like a spear to my heart. It's full of disappointment. Of regret.

Are we back to reliving the past so soon? Is this where he pulls away from me again? I turn to face the water, stifling a sob rising in my chest. Sinking onto the bench that lines the edge of the boat, I brace my hands on the warm surface. "Anyway, the email was asking me to schedule an in-person artistic review of my work." In the distance, another boat speeds past, joyful and carefree.

And here we are, stopped. Stuck. Doomed to repeat our own mistakes.

Kevin doesn't say anything for a full minute—at least. My heart is pounding so hard that I doubt I'd hear him anyway.

But then I feel his presence beside me. "I'm really proud of you, Buttercup."

My head whips around to where he's sitting, super close. "You are?"

He's wearing sunglasses, so I can't see what his eyes are telling me. But his lips … they're pulled upward. I've just told my sort-of boyfriend that I applied to attend school across the country—and he's smiling.

"Of course I am. That's huge." A hitch in his voice betrays his smile a bit. But he's trying. He's really trying. "Did you schedule the review?"

I nod. "For the second week of November, right after *The Music Man* is over."

"Will that be enough time to get your portfolio together?"

"I think so." Between the show, work at the diner, helping with my nieces, and spending time with Kevin, free time has been limited, but this is important—and we make time for the things that are important. I turn toward him, nestling myself under his arm and lifting one leg onto the bench so I can sit sideways. "So you aren't … upset?"

He places a hand on my ankle, tracing the bone absently with his thumb. "I'm not going to lie and say I'm not worried about losing you again. But if this is what you really want, I don't want to hold you back either."

I notice he doesn't say anything about making it work between us no matter what I choose. Maybe it's too early to have that discussion—especially given the fact that I haven't been admitted yet. "I might not even get in." Which would make all of this fear null and void.

He lifts his sunglasses onto the top of his head. "You'll get in."

Though he knows nothing about the design world, I love the confidence he has in me and my abilities. It's the same way I feel about him being a doctor. I know he's amazing at it, because when he gives his attention to something, he excels.

Just ask me how I know this. (Then again, a lady never kisses and tells. Wink.)

But despite the happy flutter his comment sends through me, I can't deny that this whole conversation is rather depressing. It's too early to figure out exactly what we would do if I chose to move to New York—if I did get into the program, a move wouldn't happen for ten months, anyway—so I change the subject. "Connor texted me the other day."

"He did, huh?" Kevin gets that faraway look in his eyes as he runs his fingers up and down the strap of my shirt. "And what did my brother have to say?"

"Just that he's never seen you happier and that he's rooting for us." I tilt my head. "And that he's surprised you've decided to quit attempting to get your memory back."

Kevin's hand stills.

For the last three weeks, he's been seeing a hypnotist regularly. The last I heard, they still hadn't made any progress recovering his memories. "When did you decide that?"

He shrugs. "It didn't seem to be doing any good."

"But the doctor said it might take a while, right? You can't give up so soon."

"What if …" Kevin inhales and his gaze connects with mine. "What if it's for the best that I don't remember?"

My palms tingle. "I thought you said that was the worst possible outcome. How could it be for the best?" The water laps against the sides of the boat, beating out a steady refrain as we rock.

"Sometimes"—he cradles my hand in his own, squeezes—"sometimes I'm afraid to remember. What if my memories come back and it changes things between us?"

Though it seems entirely inappropriate in this

moment, I almost want to laugh, because here we are, afraid of the same thing. "I've worried about that too."

"You have?"

Smiling, I nod. "I think we have a problem with communication, you and me."

He leans close and kisses me, then winks. "I think we do all right."

I shove his chest, just a bit, but he keeps hold of my other hand, laughing. "Kidding, kidding." Then he studies me, expression relaxed and open. "What do you mean exactly?"

How can I explain? "I've just been thinking lately about how our relationship used to be, how we weren't completely honest with each other. Maybe you held back your fears about being in a relationship because you felt guilty for being happy—" I raise my eyebrows to wait for his confirmation, and eventually he gives a gruff *hmmm*. "And I think I held back what I really wanted because I didn't want to give you any reason to walk away." Like my parents did.

I choke up a bit at that last part—because I'm not sure I even connected the dots until now.

"Aw, Buttercup." He places his hand around my shoulder and gently shifts me until I'm leaning back against him, holding onto his arm that's wrapped firmly around my middle. "I'm so sorry that I did that to you. All I can do is beg your forgiveness and promise to do better this time around."

My body is stiff at first with the tension of all the emotions, but when he says this, I sink into him. "Let's both do better this time. Maybe we can promise that we'll be completely honest, no matter how afraid we are?"

Kevin places a kiss on the back of my shoulder. "I've been given a second chance I don't deserve," he whispers. "Promising to be honest with you—to give you my everything—is the very least I can do."

Oh, how I love this man.

Still. Despite all the heartache he's put me through.

I love him.

The realization hits me like paint spatter, soaking into my soul, settling into the dry cracks of my heart. But even though I've just promised to be honest with Kevin, I don't tell him about this realization.

Because we've got time—nearly a year—to figure out how we feel.

There's literally no rush.

All the same, I don't mind showing him how I feel. So I angle my head up and back, find his lips, and do just that.

eleven

· · ·

NEW YORK ISN'T how I pictured it.

Somehow, it's more. Brighter. Bigger. Bolder. More beautiful in all its intricacies and idiosyncrasies and insights it gives into the people who live here.

People like me. Artists who find absolute joy in creating, in making clothing come alive.

I've just spent four hours in the presence of three of them. All are wonderfully diverse women who work as wardrobe interns on Broadway—the exact job that Kevin told me I should apply for back in September. After my artistic review this morning, the program director introduced me to Simone, a six-foot goddess with light brown skin, waist-length dreadlocks, and a fierce style all her own. A current student at NYU, my new Bronx-born friend showed me around and then invited me to lunch with her two roommates.

Not only was the pizza amazing, the company friendly, and the bustle of the city energizing, but the view from the pizza parlor window is to die for. It may have been chilly and rainy from the moment I opened my eyes, but that only serves to make the bright lights of Broadway brighter, the edges of the skyline sharper.

Simone smiles at me from across the red-checkered table. "Magnetic, isn't it?"

"Absolutely." I sigh. "I only wish I didn't have to go home tomorrow."

She looks at her friends—raven-haired Nadia from Romania and redheaded Ella from Scotland—who both nod. It's like some sort of girl squad code, because when Simone's attention returns to me, she lifts a dark eyebrow. "You can crash with us for an extra few days if you want."

"Really?"

But I couldn't. I've got work at the diner. Then again, Nick owes me for covering a bazillion shifts when he doesn't feel like coming in. And after a successful run last week, *The Music Man* is over and the next show doesn't begin for another week.

Then there's Kevin, who has been working like a madman. For someone who lost his memory of the last two years and hasn't gained an ounce of it back, he sure has fallen right back into a routine. But despite the fact we haven't been on a proper date since the boat outing —just a few here-or-there nights eating dinner and watching movies on the couch—he managed to sneak away to see both the opening and closing night of my show.

And we do text every day, regardless of whether we can see each other in person. When I arrived yesterday and explored the city on my own, he texted me several times for updates and I sent him silly pictures of me at various locations with a pouty face because I wished he was here with me.

So even though I miss him, I can't complain that he isn't prioritizing our relationship. All of that to say … I *could* actually stay an extra few days if I wanted to.

And I do. But I don't want to put anyone out. Maybe Simone and the girls are just being nice. "Are you sure?"

"Absolutely. We'll show you the city." Pulling her phone from inside a patchwork purse, Simone checks the time. "In fact, we've got time right now to show you our world. And there's someone you should meet."

Does she mean what I think she means? "Your world? As in …"

They all laugh as we stand. Even though it's two on a Wednesday afternoon, there's at least a half-hour's wait for a table and we fight the crowd to get out the restaurant's tiny entryway. Emerging onto 42nd Street, we enter the throng of Manhattanites coming and going. So many people, so many colors, so many interests—but somehow, all one as well.

I tug my long coat tighter and duck under an umbrella Simone offers to share while we head toward the theater where the women work. Our feet sidestep puddles as the rain beats a steady tap dance on our umbrella canopy. The women chatter about their latest show and I just drink it all in like the rainwater pooling in the alley. When they lead me down an alleyway to a stage entrance, I nearly shriek with delight—but I'm determined to be cool, on the outside at least.

Once we're inside the theater, it takes my eyes a few moments to adjust to the darkness. But with the dim lighting, the smell, the familiar hustle and bustle of backstage, I am instantly at home. This may be Broadway—and thus, a wee bit intimidating, ha!—but this is also familiar. I know this world, because it's mine.

"This way," Simone says as she presses a hand into my lower back.

The other women separate off, saying they'll see me later tonight after work. Simone and I venture down the hallway, passing open dressing rooms filled with elaborate costumes: dresses and suits, top hats and sequins and feathers, fake diamonds and tiaras. Finally, we get to an office, where Simone knocks.

A completely bald man with a goatee answers. He's got a mustard stain on his shirt and is average in every other way—average build, average height, average age. "Yeah?" With that one word, I know he's a lifer—his accent is so thick that I'd be surprised if he'd ever lived anywhere but New York.

Simone hooks a thumb in my direction. "This is the woman I told you about." She turns to me. "This is Tony Dehe, our boss."

Oh. Wow. "H-hi." I straighten, inhaling a deep breath before sticking out my hand. "Nice to meet you, sir. Lola Flanagan."

He looks me over, from head to toe—not in a creepy way, but one that's appraising me. Or maybe my style. I'm glad that I'm still wearing my go-to kick butt outfit underneath my black overcoat: yellow blazer, dark skinny jeans, and a red ruffle blouse that's feminine but not over the top. I feel both professional and extremely myself in this outfit, and I'm hoping that confidence shines through.

Because this man could someday get me a job working on Broadway.

Eek!

Finally, Tony takes my hand, gives it a one-two pump, then juts his chin toward his office. "Let's talk."

I shoot Simone a confused look and she grins, nodding while prodding me in the back. "Don't worry," she says in a low voice near my ear. "He's one of the good ones. He won't try anything shady with you."

That's a relief, though I have taken a few self-defense classes in my day just in case. I follow Tony into the office, plop into the chair across from his desk, and prepare to answer any of his questions.

An hour later, I emerge, my veins still vibrating and humming.

Simone is leaning against the wall alone. Surely she didn't wait here the whole time? She glances up from her phone and shoves it in the back pocket of her high-waisted jeans. Her black leather jacket reflects a flickering lightbulb overhead. "Well?"

I glance back into the office, but Tony is already on a phone call and not paying me one bit of attention. Stepping toward Simone, I lower my voice all the same. "He offered me a job. Like … starting next week."

Simone is not the kind of woman I pictured who would jump up and down, but right now she grips my hands and squeals—an external show of what's been brewing inside of me the last several minutes. "The moment I met you, I knew you'd be perfect to take Dani's spot."

"Who is Dani?"

"Our old roommate. She was a wardrobe assistant too until she fell in love with one of the cast. He was an understudy, and Dani got fired for tampering with the principal's costumes in an effort to get him in hot water."

My jaw drops as we move through the hallway, which has grown more crowded as the hour has grown later. "No way."

Simone's eyes flash with amusement as she stops in front of a door. "Yep. Let's just say Pierre had quite the memorable wardrobe malfunction in front of a Saturday matinee crowd. One old woman in the audience had a heart attack."

A woman in a corset and bloomers rushes past, half her hair in curlers, and she's shouting into her phone. Once she's gone, I turn my attention back to Simone. "That's terrible. Was the woman okay?"

"Oh, yeah." Simone waves her hand in the air. "Said it was the most excitement she's had in years. I heard her husband wasn't too happy to hear that."

We both laugh and I shake my head. "I still can't believe Tony just up and offered me a job—or that you recommended me for it after knowing me for half a day."

"I trust my instincts. They've helped me survive here so far." She tilts her head, and several braids swing forward over her shoulder. "Who you know is a huge part of this life. The other part is working hard. You've got to take the hardest you've ever worked in your life and then magnify it by a thousand. It can be pretty dog-eat-dog, but I like to think it's possible to do this job with integrity and kindness too. That's my method, anyway."

"Tony spoke really highly of you, and clearly he cares about your opinion. Thank you so much again."

Simone shrugs off my compliment. "So when are you moving out?"

"Oh." I tap my foot against the concrete floor. "Well, I haven't completely decided if I'll take it."

"Are you crazy? This is what you want to do, right?"

"Well, yes—"

"Then why wouldn't you be calling a moving company right now?"

I tug at my hair. "I just didn't expect to have to make this kind of decision yet." Kevin and I were supposed to have nine more months …

Though if I'm honest with myself, I know that he's the man I want to marry. So long as he keeps our relationship a priority, then I foresee a very long, lasting future with the good doctor.

But … what does that mean for my future here in the Big Apple?

"Earth to Lola." Simone taps the doorway to a costume room. "Well, hey, I don't know what to tell you except this is an amazing opportunity that you shouldn't pass up." A pause. "This is where I'm working tonight. You're welcome to stay if you'd like. Tony approved it. Maybe it will help you to see exactly what you'd be doing."

"Really? That would be amazing."

"Just don't get in the way." Arching her eyebrow, Simone spins on her heel and rushes into the room.

With a laugh, I follow her—and proceed to have the most amazing night. Yes, it's rushed and I get thrown into helping. I patch up a few rips with the sewing kit and run down the hall to find a spare shoe that will replace one that broke mid-dance number. One of the leads yells at me because I dare to sit down for one minute to catch my breath and she needs a drink of water and isn't that my job to fetch it for her? (It isn't, but that doesn't stop me from doing it anyway.)

But despite my sweaty pits and my flat hair and my disheveled clothing (I shed my blazer hours ago), I love every second of it. The thrill. Being in the presence of greatness. Seeing art come to life, actors transformed into characters.

It is the same magic I experience back home at Jenkins Theatre—but a hundred million times more exciting.

Now it's late and my feet hurt and I've just walked into my hotel room after a nightcap with Simone and the girls. While I'm changing into pajamas and brushing my teeth, my phone vibrates on the bedside table. I spit toothpaste into the sink, wash out my mouth, and hurry to slide beneath the covers.

The whole room hums with quiet, but my mind won't shut off.

I pick up the phone and glimpse a text from Theresa and another from Kevin. Before looking at the latter, I reply to my sister and let her know I'm staying until

Friday and will send her my updated flight info when I have it. Then I move on to Kevin's message. It's from earlier in the day and simply asks how the artistic review went.

I got so busy that I didn't get a chance to even tell him about Simone or Broadway. And definitely not about the job offer.

Now that I'm finally sitting still, reality pounds into me like a concrete roller. I'm flattened into dust at the idea that I have to tell him.

I know I said I'd be honest. I promised, just like he did.

But how do you tell the man you love that the mere possibility of you moving is now a highly likely event? And not just that, but that it might occur much sooner than either of you thought?

You just do. He's not the same man who rejected even the thought of you disrupting his plan. He doesn't remember that man.

Right. I open my phone to Kevin's text and dart out a reply: *Went well, I think! How about you? How was your day?*

Fine, I'm a chicken. But really, isn't it just polite to inquire after him when he asked about me?

I don't expect to hear from him since he's on shift right now, but I must have caught him on a break because I see the three-dot bubble appear under my message. It disappears, then reappears.

Maybe he's getting interrupted?

Then my phone vibrates and a green message pops up.

Kevin: *It was ... weird.*

Lola: *Care to elaborate?*

Kevin: *Um, well. My memories ... they're back.*

I sit upright in my bed and drop the phone onto the comforter like the battery is overheating. What does he mean, his memories are back?

Lola: *Like, all of them?*

Kevin: *Yeah.*

He doesn't sound happy about it. Or maybe he's just shocked.

Lola: *That's a good thing, right?*

Kevin: *It's definitely been ... enlightening.*

Just what does that mean? I'm almost too afraid to ask. Before I can, though, another message comes through—and all air leaves my lungs.

Kevin: *We should wait and talk about this when you get back. Face to face, you know?*

My fingers tingle. What is he saying? *"What if my memories come back and it changes things between us?"* The memory of our conversation from the boat rushes back and hits me between the eyes.

Is that what has happened? Has Kevin finally remembered how much better his life was the last two years once he said goodbye to me? Once he could focus solely on his career?

That has to be it. What else could he have to say to me face to face that he couldn't say over the phone except "this isn't going to work?"

The worst part? I'm not brave enough to ask—not here, alone in my hotel room. I am not strong enough to handle another heartbreak, especially three thousand miles from my support system.

My eyes blur as tears begin to fall, but somehow I manage to type out a response.

Lola: *Sure, yeah. Whatever you think is best. I'm staying here a few extra days, so I guess we can talk then.*

With trembling hands, I power down my phone before he can reply, toss it onto the side table, and flick on the hotel's television in an attempt to distract myself.

And the universe must hate me, because what do you think is on the first channel I check?

The Princess Bride.

It's the part where Buttercup pushes Westley down a hill and he says "As you wish"—and she realizes that it's not actually the Dread Pirate Roberts in front of her, but the man she loves.

Then she flings herself down the same hill in order to catch up to him, bumping and *oof*-ing all the way down.

I always thought that moment was incredibly romantic—she'd rather risk a broken neck than be without her man a second longer.

But now? I'm not sure what to think. Maybe love wasn't worth it. Maybe people really are always going to leave me. Maybe that means I need to forge my own path after all.

With a click of my finger, the TV screen goes dark— and I'm shrouded in shadows and doubts once again.

twelve

THIS IS the longest I've ever gone without turning on my phone.

For forty-eight hours, I have lived in a technology-free state of mind—except for yesterday, when I borrowed Simone's laptop to check into my flight home and shoot Theresa an email with my arrival info.

Now I'm sitting in the Phoenix airport during a three-hour layover, and my thumb rubs the sparkly pink back of my phone case. Theresa is probably going to kill me for not answering any texts she inevitably sent me, but honestly? Having my phone off has enabled me to not obsess over whether Kevin texted again.

There's a certain kind of bliss in the ignorance.

But here I am, surrounded by other travelers, and I'm only four hundred miles from reality. It's probably time to face it.

Sighing, I power my phone back on and look away while it reboots. Across from me, a young mom bounces a toddler boy on her lap while reading him a board book. A bit of applesauce from the pouch he's sucking on dribbles down his chin as he points at the book and laughs. She kisses the side of his head and coos something in his ear. It makes me miss Sami and Zoe. I can't wait to hold them when I get home—especially since I'll be leaving them in a week.

Because I took the job.

I haven't even told Theresa yet, since I just decided yesterday. She'll be happy for me, I know, but part of me still doesn't believe it's really happening.

Overhead, some gate attendant somewhere announces the boarding of yet another flight. I've been here for an hour already and have heard countless announcements—and for some reason, I find myself unable to drown them out. Maybe my subconscious is worried about missing something related to my flight.

My phone buzzes several times in my hand and, after a deep inhale, I glance down at the flood of emails and texts.

Texts from Theresa—ranging from adorable pictures of the kids to questions about how things were going in New York to texts asking WHY ARE YOU NOT ANSWERING MY MESSAGES to an acknowledgment that she received my email and will pick me up at the airport tonight.

And then there are the messages from Kevin.

Kevin: *How's New York treating you?*

Kevin: *Hey, are you okay? It's not like you to not answer my texts.*

Kevin: *Got ahold of Theresa and she gave me your flight* *info. Can I pick you up from the airport? I really need to talk to you.*

That last one was from six hours ago. Before I can change my mind, I reply with my flight info and say that yes, he can pick me up. Our talk is inevitable—we might as well get it over with so I can move on with my life.

Another announcement comes over the intercom and this time I jump. Man, my nerves are getting the better of me tonight. Standing, I sling my purse over my shoulder and wheel my carryon behind me as I walk the terrazzo floors. I dial Theresa's number and maneuver around passengers heading both directions down the concourse.

"Hey!" A baby cries in the background as Theresa answers. "Hang on. Gotta get Zoe on the boob."

"Take your time." I find a mostly empty gate and walk toward one of the large picture windows. Even though I know we're in the middle of a major metropolitan area, the view outside is fairly desolate with dust-laden concrete and brown landscape all around.

"There," Theresa huffs. "Sorry."

"No worries." I touch the window and it's lukewarm, a welcome change from New York. The brilliant cloudless sky is showing off Phoenix's gorgeous November afternoon, and I wish I could find a mountaintop and bask in the sun's rays. "I was just calling to let you know that Kevin is picking me up tonight."

"Oh, okay. I thought it was strange he wouldn't be anyway. Figured you two would want to make up for the lost time. I mean, it has been a whole four days since you saw each other." Her teasing pricks my insides, but she doesn't mean to be cruel. I haven't told her about what's going on.

"Yeah, well …"

"What's wrong?" How my sister can tell something is wrong from across the phone waves and only two words is beyond me. Then again, the woman practically raised me.

"Um." My bottom lip trembles and I focus on what's right here, what's real. My eyes find a luggage cart rumbling along just outside my window and narrow in on a bright purple suitcase. It's like a beacon, a bright spot in the desert, a reminder that good things and bad can co-exist. "I'm moving to New York."

"Wait, what? You got in?" Her excited tone must be a bit too shrill for Miss Zoe, because baby cries fill the airwaves. Theresa shushes and apologizes, coaxing her daughter to latch back on. Then, "I didn't expect you to know for several months."

"I won't." I go on to explain about Simone, meeting Tony, the job offer, and how I'll be taking over Dani's spot in the apartment.

"I'm so stinking proud of you, Lo." And I can tell— her voice wavers but the pride in it never does. "What did Kevin say?"

And, ah, there's the rub.

The worker outside my window dismounts from his seat and begins pulling suitcases off the cart, flinging them onto a conveyor belt. The purple luggage is tossed aboard and soon disappears from view.

I tap the window glass and bite the inside of my cheek. "I haven't told him yet."

"Why not?"

"Reese, he got his memories back."

"Wow." A pause. "And?"

"And … he told me in a text on Wednesday night. Then said he thought we should talk about it in person."

"Ah. And you think that means he wants to end things again?"

"What else could it mean?"

"Lots of things." She says this so matter of factly, but I don't see how.

"It's not like he doesn't have a track record for this kind of thing—leaving when things get tough. And now he has a full picture of how amazing his life was without me in it."

"You don't know that."

"Yes, I do." I turn from the window, tired of the view —of the inevitability of it. The landscape of the desert will never change, so I have to be the one to make a change.

And that's what I'm doing by moving to New York. Choosing. Not settling.

My sister is quiet a moment, and I imagine I hear baby Zoe's sweet suckling and grunts as she nurses. "Lo, what happened to trusting him?"

"It was a mistake!" I wince at the rather loud volume of my shout. Thankfully, the only person close enough to hear is a silver-haired female gate attendant who flashes me a sympathetic smile.

"So at the first sign that he might leave, you've decided to be the one to leave this time."

Darn my sister and her perceptive ways. "I thought you wanted me to move to New York. To pursue my dream."

"I do, if you're making the decision for the right reasons."

"I am." Except … well, maybe she's right. Maybe I made the decision without talking to Kevin because I'm so tired of being left behind. "Ugh."

"Look, Sis, all I'm saying is that you can't abandon a relationship at the first sign of trouble. Now, maybe it's true—maybe Kevin *is* being a complete idiot again. But maybe he's not. Don't make stupid assumptions and ruin a good thing because you're afraid to be hurt again."

I bat at a tear running down my cheek. "Did you just call me stupid?"

"No, I said your assumptions were stupid." I can hear the endearing smile in my sister's voice. "But remember when I said that love would find a way? I didn't just mean the love between you and me." She pauses again, likely to give her words time to soak into my stubborn brain. "I believe that you can have both love and your dreams. It requires a little compromise, but as long as two people focus on communicating and practicing giving lots of grace and forgiveness, then anything is possible."

"Even living three thousand miles apart?"

"Even that."

"I guess we'll see, now won't we?"

There's nothing like a quiet, non-bustling airport to agitate someone whose nerves are already fraying at the ends.

My flight was supposed to land around seven but was delayed several hours. It might have been faster to rent a car and drive home—and maybe I should have. Because then I wouldn't have to face Kevin tonight. I could have put off seeing him until I'd gotten some rest. At least I managed a stop at the bathroom to brush my hair and run wet fingers under my eyes to rid them of mascara smudges.

A girl doesn't want to *look* like she's traveled for sixteen hours when preparing to maybe get dumped. Even if she has.

As I wheel my bag down the deserted concourse just after midnight—my restroom pit stop means that nearly everyone has already hightailed it outta here before me —I try to recall my sister's words from hours ago: *"Don't make stupid assumptions and ruin a good thing because you're afraid to be hurt again."*

Right. Maybe Kevin is going to be waiting for me, freshly shaven and smiling, and all of this will have been a dumb misunderstanding on his part. If what we have is real, then the return of his memories will have changed nothing.

But the second I see him, I know that's not the case.

He's leaning forward in a seat just past the security guard stand, head in his hands, which are rubbing his face. It's like he's giving himself some sort of pep talk before he sees me. Or maybe he's just exhausted from his shift today. When I saw the flight was going to be delayed, I texted him and said I'd snag an Uber.

His response? *No, no. I need to see you.*

How was a girl supposed to take that? I want to believe it's some romantic sentiment, but maybe he just means he wants to get this over with as soon as possible so I don't take up any more space in his life.

So he can check "break up with Lola … again" off his list.

I tighten my grip on the handle of my suitcase and the wheels choose that moment to emit a high-pitched squeak.

Kevin's head whips up, revealing bloodshot eyes, an unshaven jaw, and disheveled hair that reminds me of a little boy who refuses to sit still long enough to have it sprayed and combed. Despite it being fifty-six degrees outside right now—at least, according to our pilot when we landed—he's wearing a short-sleeve T-shirt over his jeans, and goosebumps are playing hide and seek along his tan, corded forearms.

I'm not sure I've ever seen him like this, not even that day in the hospital when he fell and all of this began. Biting my cheek, I stop a few feet in front of him. "Hey."

He leaps from his seat. "Lola. H-hey." Kevin takes a step toward me, reaches for me, then hesitates. Does he just not want to fall back into old patterns, or something more? "How were your flights?"

There's a strange humming sound coming from the rafters—maybe some sort of swamp cooler or heating system. A few storefronts down, a man wearing a gray janitor's jumper wheels a sanitation cart away from us.

Other than the security guard who is probably keeping a watchful eye on us behind me, we are completely alone in this moment.

I swallow hard. "Fine."

"Good."

Oh man, how did we get back here, to the place where we can't talk to each other? We promised to be open and honest, right?

I'm too tired, too achy—in body and spirit—to delay this conversation any longer. I've got to spit out my truth before I give out completely. "I was offered a job as a wardrobe assistant on Broadway and I start next week. The interview went really well and I expect to be offered a spot in the master's program for the fall. So I'm moving. To New York."

He blinks at me, and not for the first time, I notice how long his lashes are. It takes him forever to say anything else—though I can't really blame him. I did kind of hit him hard with my truth.

"So that's it, then? You've decided?"

Somehow I know that my answer here, now, matters more than I can even comprehend. I give a firm nod. "I figured things have changed now that your memories are back." *And that I'd make the decision easier for you.* I should say that last part out loud, but I just … can't.

Tears swarm my eyes, but I blink them back. They are not welcome right now. *Later, when we're home*, I assure them internally.

And now I'm the crazy girl having a convo with her tears. Great.

"You're right." Kevin runs a hand through his hair, making it stand on end even more. "Everything *has* changed."

That's it then—I was right.

I lean heavily on the extended handle of my suitcase. "I thought it might have."

"I remember everything now." Taking another step, Kevin removes any distance between us.

My heart can't take the hot and cold, and I push against his chest. "I know. You already said that."

"I remember how I felt day after day for the last two years, knowing I'd made the biggest mistake of my life in letting you go."

Fingers fall still against his shirt. "What?"

His eyes bore into mine, pupils intense yet softened with something. Dare I hope …? "I remember how all the classic signs of lost love found me—food had no taste, accomplishments meant nothing, there was no pleasure in anything. I tried to tell myself I was fine, to throw myself into my work, but there was always something missing. You."

This can't be real. But the feel of his muscles beneath my hand—of his heart there, too—is more than real.

I don't even realize how much I have longed to hear these words until now. My Dream Man has found me again, and he and my Kevin just might be the same thing.

One of his hands skates up my arm, making me shiver until it lands on my cheek, encasing me with warmth. "When we were together the first time, I knew you were special. Knew what we had was special. Knew enough to go buy you a ring to give you someday. Knew I had never felt about anyone the way I did about you." His thumb swipes away a tear that's fallen without my permission. "But it wasn't until I lost you that I realized what real love is."

"And what is it?" My stupid voice is froggy but I don't care.

"It's you, and me, making each other better. It's you watching a movie you've seen a thousand times because you know what it means to me. It's you showing up when you didn't have to. It's you, living life beside me."

I'm full-on crying right now, clutching the soft material of his shirt. "I don't know what to do."

His eyes crinkle at the corners. "What do you mean?" He strokes my hair like it's spun gold instead of going on two days without a proper shampoo.

"I'm moving. Gave my word. And I'm excited about it, Kev. But this. You." I cup his jaw and the tiny hairs there prickle against my fingers. "So I don't know what to do. Because I love you too. But I can't stay. Not this time."

"You love me?"

"Of course I do, you dummy!" I laugh-cry, shaking my head. "Isn't it obvious? I thought you were coming here to break up with me."

His chuckle dies a quick death. "Never again." He leans in and presses a gentle kiss to my lips. A promise. "I guess all this means we'll have to do long-distance for a while."

What, until I get Broadway out of my system? I tilt my head, holding back my suspicions. "For how long?"

"Until next summer."

My nose crinkles. "What happens then?"

He smiles at me. "That's when my transfer will go through."

"Your … what?" I can't help the way my mouth hangs open. Don't even realize it until his fingers gently press my lower jaw upward.

"I spoke with my residency director. He actually knows someone at a hospital in New York and said he'd recommend me. Nothing is guaranteed, but there's a good ch—"

"You mean, you'd move?" I can't be hearing this correctly. "Give up your plan? For me?"

"Lo, I wouldn't be giving up anything. I'll still be a surgeon. Sure, my plan wouldn't look exactly as I thought it would, but that's life, right? And what is it you said about life? That its greatest treasures are found when you experience it with people you love?"

"Something like that." I lift up on my tiptoes and kiss him, smiling while I do. "I wonder why your memories came back when they did."

"I know why." His hands find my waist and press into my back, drawing me even closer. "But it's kind of embarrassing."

"Oh, really?" I throw my hands around his neck and laugh. "This I have to hear."

"Can't I just kiss you senseless and make you forget you ever asked?"

"Hmmm. Tempting. But no." I grin as I run my fingers through his thick hair. "Now spill."

His deep chuckle reverberates against me, sparking joy throughout my entire body. "Fine. If you must know, the day you left for New York, I was missing you so I …" Kevin clears his throat. "I smelled your sweatshirt."

Okay, what? That's not what I thought he was going to say—though to be fair, I really had no idea. "Come again?"

"You left your sweatshirt at my place and I love the way you always smell of honey and oranges, so I took a little whiff and bam. All my memories came flooding back."

While that's freaking adorable—and, yes, it does something simmering to my insides too—I fail to see the connection with the return of his memories. "I don't get it."

"I did the same thing night after night for months after we broke up the first time."

"You did?"

"Yes, I did." He kisses the tip of my nose. "Now that you know all of my secrets, can we please get out of here? I think that guard is wondering why we're still here and getting ready to call in the Homeland Security."

I sneak a peek over my shoulder, and the woman is

indeed standing not too far away with a grizzled look on her face, beefy arms crossed over her chest.

Giggling, I return my gaze to Kevin. "We could go tell her what we're talking about. Every detail."

Kevin groans. "Woman, you're going to be the death of me."

"Sounds like I'm going to be the life of you, actually." I sneak a kiss beneath his jaw and his grip on my waist tightens. "But yes, we can go now. After all, we've got some lost time to make up for."

I've never seen a man haul a woman down a hallway so fast, but I don't mind his caveman-like behavior—whatever life may throw at us, I'm never letting go of Kevin Bryant's hand again.

Because we are in this together. Always. Forever.

As I wish.

epilogue

. . .

Late June

A BREEZE TUMBLES off the Pacific, light and airy as it blows through the window where I'm standing in front of a floor-length mirror.

"You are a vision, my girl." Mom picks an imaginary piece of lint from my tulle dress. I wanted something simple but elegant—yet still me—and I think I've achieved it with the lacy scoop neckline and A-line dress that hugs my curves and flares into a gauzy skirt with a brush train. "I still can't believe you designed this yourself. You're so talented."

"Thanks, Mom. I'm glad you're here."

She places her arms around my waist from behind and sets her chin on my shoulder. "I wouldn't be anywhere else."

And, after months of working on our relationship, I believe her. Turns out open communication and honesty work in a parent-daughter relationship the same way they do in a romantic one. After confronting my parents about the way their abandonment made me feel—in the kindest way possible, of course—we've been able to work through the past. It's not perfect, but it's progress.

Now, here we are, staring at ourselves in the mirror inside a tiny bridal suite just off the beach where I'm going to pledge my future to Kevin. A tear rolls down my cheek.

"Stop, stop, stop!" Theresa's teal dress swishes around her knees as she rushes across the small room. When she reaches us, she shoves tissues into both of our hands. "No tears allowed until after all the photographs are taken."

"There's no way I'm not crying during the ceremony."

"Well, at least make it *there* without the waterworks."

I roll my eyes but carefully dab the corners of my eyes to preserve my makeup. "Happy?"

Theresa inspects my face before nodding. "It'll do." She cracks a smile and her own chin trembles slightly. "I'm so happy for you, Sis." Then she tugs me into a hug and my mom joins and I'm in the middle of a happy female Flanagan sandwich.

It feels good to be with my people again. The last seven months have been a whirlwind. Living in New York is amazing and working on Broadway is a dream, but it's also a ton of hard work and hasn't left as much time for Kevin and me as I'd like. But we've made it a point to talk at least once a day—whenever we can fit it into both of our schedules—and we've visited each other several times each.

During this last visit, we found our first apartment

together. I can't wait to move in when we return from our honeymoon to the Cayman Islands. Kevin will join me when his new residency starts in the fall, right around the same time as my grad program begins.

A tornado of blonde curls and a small white dress that matches my own burst through the doorway. "Auntie Lo, Uncle Kevin says he wants to see you nooooow!"

Even though it's only four in the afternoon and the wedding cake has yet to be served, someone has clearly given Sami lots of sugar because she won't stop bouncing up and down. My bet is on Simone, who saunters in after my niece grinning. We've become really close and, though I cannot wait to live with Kevin, it'll be sad to not be in the same apartment as my new best friend. Thankfully, I'll see her both at school and work, so there will still be lots of time to spend making memories together.

Our photographer, a dark-haired woman in black, ducks inside too. Even though she's been taking photos of us all morning—first shots of me alone by the water, then of me with the girls—the whir and click of her camera fill the room.

I squat to Sami's level and gently tug on a piece of her hair. She's wearing it down and curled, flowing free just like mine. "He does now, does he?"

"Mm-hmm." Her eyes are wide as she reaches out to touch the delicate crown of flowers topping my head. "I think you'd better go see him now."

"Should we get this show on the road, then?"

"Yes!" Sami pumps a fist and we all laugh as she

rushes to the box the florist dropped off earlier and snags her flower girl basket filled with red rose petals.

My heart thumps and sings as Theresa hands me my simple bouquet of calla lilies. We link arms and walk through the doorway and out into the sunshine. The clouds that earlier provided fabulous lighting for photos have dissipated, leaving behind a pure sapphire sky.

Wedding chairs are set up a little way down the beach, and four men stand just below an arch adorned with flowers in an array of bright pinks, yellows, and blues. Though I can't make out very many details from where I'm standing, I immediately know which one is Kevin. He's pacing in front of the preacher, and the guy next to him—Connor, I think—places a hand on his shoulder.

Is my soon-to-be-husband nervous? Or just as anxious as I am to finally be man and wife?

My dad joins us and kisses my cheek. "Ready, Lola?" He's a man of few words, but I know that he loves me and thinks I'm beautiful. I can see it in his green eyes.

"Yes, Daddy." *More than ready.*

I press forward, my bare toes sinking into the warm, sun-kissed sand. The water laps the shore, bringing with it the familiar swish and tug of the summer breeze. As I get closer, my heart slows along with time. Music lilts on the air—the *Princess Bride* theme song—and now I'm close enough to see Kevin for real.

Sweet Moses, he's handsome with his jaw freshly shaven, hair freshly cut, and he's wearing a linen khaki suit with an unbuttoned jacket, white notched lapel shirt, and no tie.

Connor escorts my mom to her seat up front next to Jake, who is holding baby Zoe in his lap. We've kept our ceremony fairly small and intimate—just family and some close friends—and chatter rises around us as they all realize we're getting ready to begin.

Kevin's eyes find me quick and my stomach erupts into a thousand fireflies, lit and dancing inside me. When he mouths, "I love you," I nearly break Theresa's no crying rule.

Simone walks down the aisle first, then Theresa, then Sami, whose triumphant tosses into the air leave the crowd in stitches. Everything from there happens in both slow and flash motion—some things I know I'll remember, others that will have to be captured via photo or video. There's just so much going on, but all I can see is Kevin.

When at last my dad walks me down the short aisle, I find myself in front of my true love. Dad gives me away and Kevin and I step up to the pastor.

Who clears his throat, lifts a bushy gray eyebrow and says, "Mawwage. Mawwage is what bwings us together today."

And because I had no idea he was going to be quoting *The Princess Bride*, I am that oh-so-sophisticated bride who snorts a laugh. Kevin's eyes are twinkling and I can't believe he's changed so much from the straight-laced doctor who took everything seriously to someone who plays a tiny prank on his wedding day.

The rest of the ceremony is smooth sailing from there as we say our vows and place rings on each other's fingers—well, smooth until the unity candle won't light thanks to the breeze's blustering. But we laugh it off and return to facing each other, and then the pastor tells us that we're officially married. "Kevin, you may kiss your bride."

Connor and Kevin's other groomsman hoot and whistle, and the audience joins in. With a grin, Kevin steps toward me and lowers his mouth toward mine, kissing me sweetly with just a hint of the passion I know he's saving for tonight. When he steps away, we lift our hands together and I shout, "Woo hoo!"

Our procession down the aisle is short and sweet and ends in another kiss, this one more fiery but ending too soon as our wedding party descends on us with hugs and congrats.

Connor is the last one to approach us. The emotion on his face is real as he tugs Kev into a brotherly hug and pats his back hard. "Mom would have loved this."

"Thanks, bro."

Then Connor turns to me and slips me into an embrace. "She would have loved you too."

"Aw." I pull away and let the tears finally come as I reach into my bouquet for the blue handkerchief that belonged to the mother-in-law I never knew. "I can't wait to meet the woman who finally catches your eye, Connor. No doubt your mom would have loved her too."

A look comes over his face, half grimace, half wistfulness. Then he laughs and shakes his head. "I think it's perpetual bachelorhood for me."

He might be right, if his date for this evening—a different one than the woman he brought to the rehearsal dinner last night—is any indication. (No offense to her, but the girl is as fake as they come, both personality wise and physically, if you catch my drift.)

But I still have hope that he'll find a great girl someday.

As if he's reading my mind, Kevin claps Connor on the shoulder. "Watch out, man. Someday, you'll meet an amazing woman who will stop you in your tracks and make you see things differently. Just look at me." He presses a kiss against my temple and I rest against him, my arms around his waist.

"It's a nice thought." Connor tugs at the top button of his shirt and looks off into the distance. "But according to Dad, I'll never be as good as you, so why even try?" Then with a demeaning chuckle, he saunters off toward his date, who is taking duck-faced selfies of herself under the wedding arch.

Kevin looks down at me. "I worry about him."

"Don't. He'll find his way. Like you said, just look at you."

"True. If I was living out my way, I'd still be planning a life in San Diego. Eating takeout all alone every night."

I twist so we're face to face, my arms still around him and his around me. "Instead, you'll be eating takeout with me by your side."

He laughs. "One of us should probably figure out that cooking thing, huh?"

"Probably. Or we both could. Maybe cooking lessons?" Giving him a saucy look, I tilt my head and bite my lip. "Then again, our time together will be pretty limited in the near future … and I think there are other ways we might want to spend it."

"Oh, really?" The irises of his eyes darken and a lazy smile takes over his face. "And what are those, wife?"

"You'll just have to be patient and find out, husband."

"Patience is not a virtue I possess. But for you, I would do anything." His mouth lingers just above mine. "I love you, Buttercup. Never doubt it."

"I will never doubt again."

He smiles at my excellent use of a *Princess Bride* quote and replies in kind. "There will never be a need."

And to prove it, he seals his promise with a kiss.

Thank you so much for joining Lola and Kevin on their journey back to love. Now that they've found theirs, we've got to give Connor his happily ever after, don't you think?

If you agree, check out *Loving the Ladies' Man*, available in e-book, paperback, and audio.

Loving the Ladies' Man

I have exactly three months, two weeks, and one day until my life potentially changes forever.

And my mother won't let me forget it.

She doesn't mean to make me feel guilty. I know that. But whenever I talk with her, I can't help but think about the approaching deadline—about the promise I made nearly a decade ago.

"I know you love California, Evie, but I just couldn't live there." We're shooting the breeze, catching up over my lunch break while I sit behind my desk eating cold leftover pizza. She's spent the last several minutes telling me about all the things that have happened this week on the Iowa dairy farm she runs with my dad— the one that's been in the Denmark family for over a century. The one I left behind to follow my own dreams. "I'd miss the rolling plains, the four seasons, the peace and quiet of home."

As I hold my phone to my ear, I take a bite of crust

and swivel in my office chair, leaning back and looking up at the familiar ceiling that's riddled with a crumbly popcorn texture and several cracks. "Actually, I kind of like the fact that it's February and I'm not freezing my rear off." I try to infuse lightness into my tone, but can't help the way it notches up, tight. "And not sure I'd exactly call it quiet there with all of those mooing cows."

"Oh, sugar." She laughs, and I can hear in her voice how much she loves me. "We sure do miss you. It's not the same without you here. Maybe you can come for a visit soon?"

"Sure, Mom. I'll try." And I feel it again, like I'm sinking, drowning in a sea of *should-I-have*s. There's nothing I hate more than hearing the disappointment in my mother's voice.

But I know it isn't just disappointment—it's need. My parents *need* me to hold up my end of the bargain. The tiny bit of money I've started sending home every month isn't enough to make much of a difference. Definitely not enough to hire another employee to give my parents a break.

Looking back, I suppose it was short-sighted to tell my parents I would move home and take over the dairy farm—the job I was groomed for since I was a kid—if I hadn't met a certain level of career success within ten years. It was even more short-sighted to define "success" as "sending home X amount of dollars every month." I cringe to think of that now, as if my self-worth can be tied to my finances.

But back then, ten years felt like a lifetime. I thought I had all the time in the world to prove to my parents—

to myself—that I could both pursue my passions *and* be the daughter they deserved.

There's a knock on my door and I sit up straight. Sally, one of my acquisitions editors, is standing in my office doorway. She waves at me and her eyes widen in that "I've got something important to discuss" look.

I hold up a finger and lower my voice. "Sorry, Mom. I've got to go."

"Of course, sweetie. Talk soon?"

"Yes. Soon." I hang up, blow out a breath, and run my hands through my waist-length brown hair that desperately needs a wash—and a trim.

But as the editorial director at Evermore Publishers, a boutique press in San Diego, I don't have time for things like haircuts. I've been working about twelve to fifteen hours every day for the last two years—ever since David broke my heart—trying to prove to my boss that I'm a valuable employee so that when a promotion finally comes along, I'm in the running.

Plus, work has been a helpful way to forget the searing loss of my ex—the one that took me by complete surprise, even though it probably shouldn't have.

I wonder if it'll help me forget the stupid wedding invitation that showed up in the mail last week …

Ugh. *Focus, Evie.*

"Hi, Sally." I wave her into the office. "What's up?"

The twenty-something ducks inside and slides into the chair on the other side of my desk. "Sorry to interrupt. But …" She tugs on the ends of her black bob. That's when I notice her eyes are bloodshot, her bottom lip trembling.

"Hey." I reach for a tissue and hand it to her. "What's going on?"

With a brave smile, she takes the tissue and wads it up into her fist. "It's just that ..." Her voice wobbles. "I'm a bit behind on the Perry project. I'd intended to work all weekend to finish it before Monday's deadline but ..." And then she starts to cry.

I jump out of my seat and round the desk, pulling my wheeled office chair with me. Then I sit and put an arm around her.

I know it's not in my job description, but I can't help but feel like my team is my family. Like Sally—along with Justine, Kelly, and Tanya—are my younger sisters. And I've got to do whatever it takes to help them succeed. To protect them. To keep them close.

And when I say it out loud, I realize I sound like a crazy person. Because these women, though younger than me, are adults and don't need their manager taking care of them. But it doesn't take a shrink to figure out that this intense need to make sure my team is okay stems from the fact that I didn't protect my own sister, once upon a time.

I squeeze Sally's shoulders again. "But what?"

"Well, the story is so beautiful and I've loved working on it, but John just ..." Her breath is coming in spurts now. "He just broke up with me yesterday, and I can't—absolutely can't—bring myself to keep working on a story that's got a happy ending. Not right now."

"I can understand how that would be really diffi-cult." John ... Wait, John? I thought her boyfriend was named Steve or something like that. "How long were you together?"

"T-two whole weeks!" Sally blows her red nose into the tissue. Mascara is now running down her cheeks and she looks like some sort of creepy clown.

I let her cry for a few more minutes while I rub her back. Because I understand this, the heartache of losing someone you love. Sure, some would say that two weeks is nothing compared to the years I invested in my relationship with David. But if you think someone is the one, and it turns out he isn't, it doesn't matter how long you were together. It hurts.

So it stands to reason that Sally might be hurting just as much as I did. Who am I to judge? "What can I do to help?" I mentally scan our editorial schedule. "We could maybe extend the deadline by a few days."

Sally shakes her head vehemently. "I don't think that will help. I … I can't work on any romances right now."

"But …" Evermore solely publishes romantic fiction. There are literally no other projects I *can* give her. "What do you suggest?"

She peeks up at me. "Could I take some time off next week? It would be really helpful for me to visit my family in Los Angeles. You understand, don't you? Family is so important."

Sure, drive the knife in deeper, Sally. Of course, she doesn't know all the ways I'm currently failing my own family. "Yes, that's absolutely fine. You have some vacation days, right?"

There she goes biting her lip again. "Maybe one or two."

I hold back a sigh. "That's fine. I'll approve the extra time."

"Oh, thank you so much." She throws her arms around my neck for a quick hug. But then she pulls back, brow furrowed. "What about the Perry project?"

"Don't worry about it. Just email me your notes so far." I guess I'll be spending my evening buried in the historical love story of Lady Elizabeth Williams and Lord Isaac Fairfax. There are worse ways to spend my time—she's right that it's a beautiful book, and from one of our more seasoned authors—but I was really looking forward to a movie night at home with my four house-mates. It's taken us weeks to find a night that will work with all of our schedules and now I get to be the one to disappoint my friends.

My stomach tightens just thinking about it.

Sally stands and wipes away the residual mascara on her face. She suddenly seems much more chipper, lighter, even. "Oh, by the way, Lisa said she needed to see you."

"All right." What could my boss want? Normally, she just sends me an IM or email if she wants an update on a project. "Thanks."

"No problem." Sally turns and fairly skips from the room. Just the thought of seeing her family must be enough to make her feel better.

I lock my computer and head out of my tiny office into the hallway with blue carpet that has to have been around longer than I've been alive (and do I want to know what kind of dirt and germs are embedded in the carpet that's more than thirty-two years old? No, I do not). I arrive at Lisa's door, knock, and pop my head inside her office.

Lisa Chambers—Evermore's publisher (aka, head honcho)—is standing beside the large picture window that gives a picturesque view of downtown San Diego several miles away. Our office may be ancient and located in an out-of-the-way, decrepit business complex abutting a mountain, but it offers the most fantastic views you can imagine.

"Hi." I attempt to straighten my rumpled cotton skirt, which is a bit crooked from my quick walk over. "Sorry, I just heard you needed to see me."

Lisa waves her hand. "Not a problem. Come on in." Today her silver-threaded hair is pulled back into a bun, which makes her high cheekbones even more pronounced than usual. She's a five-foot-three power-house in a silky emerald-green blouse, a black jacket with three-quarter sleeves, and sleek black pants that probably cost more than I make in a month.

As I sit in one of the leather chairs across from her broad oak desk, I double check my white blouse to ensure Sally's mascara didn't stain it. Whew. All clear.

I cross and then uncross my legs. "So, all of our projects are on track to meet deadlines. As you know, we've just acquired two new titles and I'm very excited about one in particular." Lisa stays quiet, just keeps staring out the window, so that must not be what she wants to discuss. Is she leaving it up to me to figure it out? She does that sometimes, and I hate it. I clear my throat. "Is this a good time to ask about the budget meeting yesterday? Because I was a bit confused by the—"

"Evie." Lisa turns from the window, wearing an amused look. "Breathe."

"Right." I close my eyes for a minute, inhaling, imagining myself doing yoga. But who am I kidding? Yoga is totally Kayla and Lauren's thing. The one time they dragged me along to yoga on the beach, I ended up with a bloody nose after a downward-facing dog pose went awry.

"Sorry I'm late."

My eyes pop open at the deep male voice that suddenly reverberates through the room. I smell Connor before I see him, his citrusy cologne with hints of cedarwood and bergamot making my toes curl of their own accord inside my low-heeled pumps.

Marketing director Connor Bryant breezes through the door and sits in the chair next to me. I peek at him from the corner of my eye. A man should not be allowed to be as sexy as he is, with that brown hair styled to perfection and that five o'clock scruff dusting his tan, chiseled jaw. His black designer-cut suit fits him like a glove, serving to outline the broad shoulders of a guy who has clearly been an athlete all his life.

If I were ever to see him with his shirt off—*don't even picture it, Evie!*—he would definitely have a six-pack lurking under the crisp dark blue shirt that brings out the piercing quality of his gold-flecked brown eyes.

Too bad his sexiness is only skin deep.

Oh, plenty of women in our office, from Kim in accounting to Chelsea in sales to Bridgette in legal, rave about Connor's personality too. (*"He's the whole package, you guys!"*) I don't know if the rumors are true that he's gone to drinks (and done who knows what else) with several of the women in the office, but he obviously enjoys his position as the only male at Evermore excepting seventy-year-old Jorge in subsidiary rights.

So yeah, Connor may have a pretty face, but when I look at him, I just see a ginormous flirt who leads women on—and I despise a man like that.

Especially when he keeps a woman on the hook for years. When he makes her think he's just as into her as she is him. When the whole time he's dating her, he is actually falling for her friend.

Oh, wait. I was talking about Connor, wasn't I?

Not David.

Still. Men like him can't be trusted.

Connor lifts his stupidly sexy eyes in acknowledgment of me for a split second before turning a crooked grin toward Lisa. "To what do we owe the pleasure of your summons, oh Fearless Leader?"

Here we go.

But instead of rolling my eyes at his sweet talk like I really want to do, I act the professional and flit on a smile to match his, straightening in my seat as if that will make me more than the frumpy workaholic he must see me as. "Yes, Lisa, can't wait to hear what all of this is about!"

Connor snorts at my peppy timbre, but I ignore him and keep focused on Lisa, who finally sits and places her folded hands on the desktop. My heart skitters in that moment. It's not abnormal for her to meet with

Connor and me at the same time, but this meeting was unscheduled.

Unplanned.

And I absolutely hate it when things are sprung on me. My mind flashes to the invitation tucked under a stack of papers on my desk back in my office. *Stephanie Lamb and David Atkinson invite you to join their wedding celebration …*

I shudder and refocus on Lisa, whose lips are moving. Oh no. I missed whatever it is she said.

"… and that's why I've narrowed down my pool of contenders to the two of you."

Huh? Contenders for what?

My eyes dart between Lisa and Connor, who strokes his long fingers down the sides of his face and chin. "Thank you for having such faith in us, Lisa. We won't let you down."

When both of their gazes float in my direction, I nod, a tad too enthusiastic (especially for someone who has no idea what was said). But there's no way I can admit I wasn't listening. "Absolutely."

"Wonderful. So I'll be watching you both even more closely." Lisa turns to face her computer, then flicks her eyes back to us. "Go on, then. Back to work, my dream team."

Connor stands and I follow suit, all the way into the hallway. Before he can return to his office, I place my hand on his upper arm. And *ho boy*. His bicep underneath my fingers is rock hard. I know he works as much as I do, so how in the world does this guy find time to get arms like *this*? Maybe he does pushups in his office in between conference calls.

My armpits are suddenly sweating at the mental image.

"Yeah?" His six-two frame doesn't exactly tower over me—after all, I'm five-nine. But I feel as small as a mouse facing a mountain when I look up into those same eyes that are every woman's fantasy.

Every *other* woman, that is.

I quickly remove my hand. "So I was a bit distracted in there." Flexing the fingers that just touched Connor, I rub them with my other hand. "I didn't hear what Lisa said."

"Which part?" Arms crossed over his chest, he leans against the hallway wall, regarding me with an air of coolness—his *modus operandi* when it comes to our interactions in private.

"Um … all of it?"

He laughs, incredulous.

Why did I ever think to ask him for help? "Forget it. I'll just …" Sure that my face resembles a tomato, I turn on my heel to retreat to my office.

"Wait."

I stop, pivot back to face him, eyebrows raised.

He runs a hand through his hair. Lucky hand. (*Stop it, Evie! So he's attractive! Get over it.*) "She said that she's opening up an associate publisher position around Memorial Day—when the budget will allow for it—and she wants to promote from within."

Associate publisher would be a significant step up for me. More responsibilities, little to no editing, but it would come with better benefits, including a larger paycheck.

Exactly what I need to finally fulfill the promise I made to my parents.

And just in time too, because Memorial Day is about three months away.

I tap my foot against the ground. "And she's going to promote one of us?"

"That's right." A tiny smile curls the edges of his lips.

What? Does he think he's got the job in the bag? I mean, yeah, if Lisa is selecting someone based on how well they can schmooze, Connor will for sure be her top pick.

But I work just as hard, if not harder, than he does. My team seems to like me all right. I know the business inside and out. And I'm a darn good editor.

Yes. I'd be a good choice too.

That's right, Evie. Keep telling yourself you have a chance against Mr. Charming.

I swallow hard. "So one of us will become the other's boss?" Just what I need—and I don't know which scenario would be worse. Somehow having to manage Connor or having a boss I don't respect.

"She was a bit murky on those details. Said most likely she'd keep at least one of our positions as a direct report for herself. She just needs someone to share the load."

Whew. Tugging at the bottom of my shirt, I nod. "Thanks for filling me in."

"Of course." He studies me for a moment, then extends his hand. "May the best person win."

"Right." When I touch his skin with my own, something in my legs becomes soft, like melting ice. And yet Connor doesn't seem affected at all. He pulls his hand away and turns back toward his office.

Just as I'm retreating into my own, I hear him greet our receptionist, June. He's over-the-top friendly and I turn my head at the last minute to see him leaning over her desk, plucking a piece of chocolate from her dish and laughing when she punches him playfully in the shoulder.

In the ten years that we've worked together, he's never once acted like that with me. In fact, other than Lisa, I might just be the only woman in the office he's never flirted with.

But you know what? That's fine. I mean, at one point, I might have welcomed his attention (back when I was naive). But then I had David, and that relationship consumed me for three years.

And if David taught me anything, it's that I can't trust my own judgment when it comes to smooth-talking men.

Now, I'm focusing on my career—either I'll get this job and stay here in California, or Connor will get promoted and I'll get a one-way ticket back to Iowa, having failed in my mission to send my parents enough money for the farm.

Sure, my dream job will be in the rearview mirror, but at least they won't have to suffer anymore for their daughter's selfish choices.

I've already cost them their oldest daughter. I can't cost them their livelihood—their home—as well.

Blinking against hot liquid threatening to fall down my cheeks, I peel my eyes off of the scene unfolding in the front lobby and step firmly into my office, closing the door and plopping into my chair.

As I wake up the computer screen, download Sally's notes, and put my eyes on the historical manuscript she sent over, I slowly lose myself in the story. My breath comes easier and my pulse slows.

And yet, in the back of my mind, there pounds a steady thought.

Somehow, I have to beat Connor—but I don't know if I can.

books by kristin canary

California Dreamin' Series

Enamoring Her Amnesic Ex (prequel)

Loving the Ladies' Man

Desiring His Dating Coach

Saving the Secret Prince

Belonging With Her Best Friend

Engaging the Office Enemy

Needing the Next-Door Neighbor

Hallmark Beach Series

Beachside Kisses With My Bodyguard

about the author

Kristin is a wife and boy mom who functions best on peach tea and cookie dough ice cream. A desert dweller, she always has her eye on the next trip to a beach somewhere—and if she can't travel there in person, then you'd better believe she's going to write about it. Kristin is never fully satisfied with a movie, TV show, or book without a hefty dose of romance in it, and she's grateful to be living a true-life love story with her own crazy little family. Connect with her at KristinCanary.com.

 facebook.com/kristincanary

 instagram.com/kristincanaryauthor